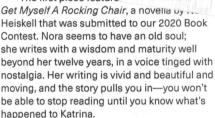

StoneSoup
Writing and art by kids, for kids

Editor's Note

I am so excited to share two pieces of fiction with you this summer.

The first piece features *Before I Get Myself A Rocking Chair*, a novella by Nora Heiskell that was submitted to our 2020 Book Contest. Nora seems to have an old soul; she writes with a wisdom and maturity well beyond her twelve years, in a voice tinged with nostalgia. Her writing is vivid and beautiful and moving, and the story pulls you in—you won't be able to stop reading until you know what's happened to Katrina.

In this issue you'll also find an excerpt from *The Other Realm* by Tristan Hui, the winner of our 2020 Book Contest, which you can preorder now at our store—it comes out on September 1st! Tristan's novel tells the story of Azalea Morroe, and her epic journey across a haunted desert. It's an adventure story with a huge heart that will also make you laugh! I hope you enjoy reading the first few chapters, and I'm so excited to share the full novel with you in September.

In the meantime, I encourage all of you to submit to our 2021 Book Contest! This year, we will select one winning novel and one winning poetry manuscript, though we consider all entries for potential publication in the magazine. The contest closes on August 16, 2021.

On the cover:
By the Glow of a Thousand Candles (Canon XS600)
Sage Millen, 13
Vancouver, British Columbia, Canada

Editor in Chief
[...]

Managing Editor
Jane Levi

Blog & Special Projects
Sarah Ainsworth

Design
Joe Ewart

Stone Soup (ISSN 0094 579X) is published eleven times per year—monthly, with a combined July/August summer issue. Copyright © 2021 by the Children's Art Foundation–Stone Soup Inc., a 501(c)(3) nonprofit organization located in Santa Cruz, California. All rights reserved.

Thirty-five percent of our subscription price is tax-deductible. Make a donation at Stonesoup. com/donate, and support us by choosing Children's Art Foundation as your Amazon Smile charity.

POSTMASTER: Send address changes to Stone Soup, 126 Otis Street, Santa Cruz, CA 95060. Periodicals postage paid at Santa Cruz, California, and additional offices.

Stone Soup is available in different formats to persons who have trouble seeing or reading the print or online editions. To request the braille edition from the National Library of Congress, call +1 800-424-8567. To request access to the audio edition via the National Federation of the Blind's NFB-NEWSLINE®, call +1 866-504-7300, or visit Nfbnewsline.org.

Submit your stories, poems, art, and letters to the editor via Stonesoup.submittable.com/submit. Subscribe to the print and digital editions at Stonesoup.com. Email questions about your subscription to Subscriptions@stonesoup.com. All other queries via email to Stonesoup@stonesoup.com.

Check us out on social media:

Stone Soup

Contents

ART

Wooden Sunset (iPhone 11)
Amelia Driver, 10
Woodacre, CA

Get Myself a Rocking Chair

Katrina's life changes when she starts visiting Mr. McCumber, a lonely old man with no family of his own

By Nora Heiskell, 12
Philadelphia, PA

Chapter One

*Lord I been hangin' out of town in
that low-down rain
Watchin' good-time Charlie, friend,
is drivin' me insane
Down on shady Charlotte Street,
the green lights look red
Wish I was back home on the farm,
in my feather bed*

The soft music of the guitar floated through the still air. Smoke from a chimney could be seen above the rooftops of town.

Peter McCumber was an odd man. He spoke to no one, but he sang and played his guitar as if he was all alone in his own world. Nobody could remember the last time Peter McCumber had gone to church, let alone to visit somebody. The townspeople all kept their distance, as if he were ill or crazy or something. My father was the only person that would speak to him.

I was interested in the old man; there were not many elderly people in Emerald Hills, where we lived. The only other one was Mrs. Gaffney, the milliner. But, like everyone else, I kept my distance.

Our town, Emerald Hills, consisted of two neighborhoods. I lived at the very edge of the smaller neighborhood, closer to the part of town where all the shops were. My house was a tiny one-story cottage with whitewashed boards and sky-blue trim around the windows. I lived with my father and our cook, Helen. My mother died when I was only four, and I hardly remembered her. Helen came shortly after Mother died, and she had raised me for most of my life.

I opened the kitchen door, and a wave of delicious scents hit me. Helen hardly ever made anything hot in the summertime, but today was Friday, and Grandmother was coming. Helen had cooked a whole chicken and made mashed potatoes, which were a special treat. She had roasted carrots and for dessert there was a large chocolate cake hidden in the cupboard.

"Smells delicious!" I exclaimed, dropping into a chair.

"It's nothing," Helen said with a smile. "But I could use some help. Go change and then help me set the table."

"Sure." I left the kitchen and went into my bedroom. I picked out the blue dress Father got me for my birthday. It was very lovely, but I hated dresses, and I wore overalls almost every day. But I knew that Father would appreciate it if I dressed nicely tonight because Grandmother was coming.

My father's parents had died before I was born, but my mother's mother was still alive. She was a stately old lady, and very old-fashioned. She did not really approve of my father, because my mother had run away to marry him. But with time she had grown to tolerate him, and after Mother died, she helped us in some small ways.

Anyway, Grandmother did not approve of girls wearing pants, so every time she came, I donned a dress and stuffed my overalls to the back of my closet, in case she happened to peek in.

The dining room was set up nicely with a pale yellow tablecloth and flickering candles. Usually, we ate at the kitchen table, but as I've said, Grandmother was very stately and old-fashioned and did not approve of dining in the kitchen.

I helped Helen bring the various dishes to the table. Just as we finished, the front door opened and my father entered.

I could hear him taking off his hat and putting down his umbrella.

He had been in the city, picking up Grandmother. I ran to him and wrapped my arms around him. "Hey, kiddo. How was your day?" he asked, squeezing me to him.

"Good," I told him. Then I heard a loud sniff.

I stepped away from Father to see Grandmother standing beside him. She was very short, not much taller than me, but Father once said that was a good thing, because if she were any taller, she would be too intimidating to even talk to.

"Hello, Grandmother," I said quietly.

She sniffed again. "It is not proper to come flying at someone like that. And Martin, you must not say 'hey'— it's so unrefined! When I was young, we stood in a line in front of my father when he came home from work, so as to greet him. We never flew at him like small animals!" she said.

That is what I meant about Grandmother.

Father smiled. "Katrina was just happy to see me. That's all," he said.

"Yes, well." She sniffed again. "*Really*, Martin. I do think you should have named her Julia Margaret! That's proper, you know! The first daughter named for her mother! Especially because her mother is now dead. Did you ever think about changing her name after my daughter died? It would make people see how much you were mourning her!"

Grandmother brought this up every time she visited. But Father always said with his quiet firmness that my mother had hated the name Julia Margaret and had not wanted to name her daughter that.

"Supper's going to get cold. Why don't we all head into the dining room and have a bite to eat?" suggested Helen, poking her head through the door.

"And *really*, Martin. Servants should know their place! They should not interrupt conversations! They should not talk at all!" Grandmother said.

"Helen is a dear friend, not a servant," Father replied. He still spoke in the same calm manner that he always did, but I could tell he was aggravated.

Helen did not seem to mind Grandmother's remarks. I saw her hiding a smile as she withdrew back into the dining room.

Dinner was mostly uneventful. Grandmother criticized everything from peeling paint on the walls to how Father's wristwatch was seven seconds faster than the grandfather clock in the corner.

All the food was delicious, and so was the cake that Helen brought out after everyone had cleared their plates. Helen did not say another word throughout the rest of the meal. Of course, Grandmother had said that was the proper behavior for a "servant," but I think she knew Helen was secretly laughing at her.

After dinner, Grandmother retired to the bedroom that was usually Helen's. There were only three bedrooms in our house, so Helen would be sleeping in with me that night. "How Meg could be who she was when her mother is like that . . ."

Father muttered as he helped Helen and I clear the table. Indeed, I hardly remembered my mother, but Father had told me stories about her, and it seemed like she and her mother were polar opposites. We went out onto the front porch after dinner was cleaned up. We often did this in the summertime, because it was too hot to go to bed right after dinner, and the sun was still up.

"I got a letter from my daughter this afternoon," Helen said suddenly. "She is going to have a baby."

"Why Helen, that is wonderful! Do you know when the baby is to come?" Father asked.

"In September."

There was little else to say, so we sat in silence for a long while, watching the sky change from blue to periwinkle to violet and then finally, an inky blue. The stars appeared one by one, as if someone were lighting hundreds of candles to cut through the darkness. I leaned against my father's strong shoulder and closed my eyes.

I think that I fell asleep against Father's shoulder, because he woke me and I stumbled blearily into bed. The last thing that I remembered were the soft notes of a guitar and an old man's voice echoing across the quiet town.

Found myself a picker friend
who's read yesterday's news
Folded up page twenty-one and
stuck it in my shoe
Gave a nickel to the poor,
my good turn for the day
Folded up my own little folder
and threw it far away

Chapter Two

The next day was Saturday, and early in the morning, before Helen or I were awake, Father took Grandmother back to the city and then came back home. He arrived at the crack of dawn, just as Helen and I were getting up to start breakfast.

There was lots of work to do on Saturdays, so we were apt to be up earlier that day than any other day of the week. Helen insisted that we clean the entire cottage, top to bottom, every Saturday. Then, we had to make little snacks for after church the next day while Father prepared the sermon. He was the minister.

But that day, as we were sitting down to breakfast, Father came out with a new idea. "What do you say you come with me to visit Mr. McCumber today?" he asked. "I haven't visited him in a long time, and I think he might like to have a new visitor," he said. "I-I'm not sure he would," I said quietly. "He doesn't talk to anyone. Maybe he wouldn't like a strange girl coming to visit him without being asked."

Father chuckled. "I actually think he would like that. But if you don't want to go, I understand."

"I could use your help around here too. There's lots of things to be done today," Helen added.

I smiled at her, then turned to Father. "I think I'd like to come," I said.

Helen laughed. "I guess meeting mysterious old men is more fun than cleaning the house with an old widow," she said.

"No—it's not like that!" I said quickly, but she laughed again.

"Only teasing."

I gave her another smile, then took a bite of scrambled eggs.

Peter McCumber's house was on Orchard Street, only two blocks away from our house. His house was about the same size as ours, but it didn't look so welcoming. The roof was sagging over the back, and the whole thing had an air of old age and loneliness.

Father went up and knocked on the door. I hung back a little, nervously. The door opened a crack, and a weathered, lined face peeked out.

"Mr. McCumber?" Father said.

Mr. McCumber grunted, then shut the door and stepped out onto the porch. He sat down in a rocking chair, and gestured to two stools sitting side by side. I sat down on one of the stools and Father took the other.

"Who's she?" he asked, looking at my boots.

"This is my daughter, Katrina," said Father.

"Why's she here?" he demanded.

"Because I asked her to come along today and she has obliged," Father responded patiently.

Mr. McCumber grunted again.

There was a bit of an awkward silence. Then Father spoke.

"Did you have a favorite out of one of the books I gave you last week?"

Mr. McCumber grunted again. It seemed that, though he liked to sing, he did not like to speak. Father held out the stack of books he had brought along.

"Here. These were the ones you asked me for, right?"

Mr. McCumber just grunted, but he took the books with a nod of gratitude.

"Well, we best be going," Father said, a little uncomfortably. "I'll see you later."

We were about to leave when Mr. McCumber finally spoke. "If she'd like to, your little girl can come around whenever she pleases. I'd like to have her."

Father nodded and stood up. It had been a very short visit, but I was ready for it to be over.

"Father, why did Mr. McCumber ask for me to come back if he never spoke to me?" I asked as we approached our house.

"Mr. McCumber is not your normal man. He lost his entire family during the war. He has been stricken by grief ever since, and the people who knew him before say that he was never the same again. I think that you might remind him of his own little daughter. She was your age when she died. If it would be okay with you, I think that you should go and see him."

"He's . . . different. I'm not sure I want to go back."

"I know what you mean. I tried to visit Mr. McCumber many times, and he always shut the door in my face. But one day he left the door open. I don't think Mr. McCumber would appreciate you coming out of pity, but I think the two of you could be friends. The reason he finally opened the door to me was because I told him about how I lost your mother. He knew that I understood his grief. I know you hardly remember your mother, but I think that you might be able to connect through something else."

"I guess." I still wasn't so sure.

"Just think about it."

I stayed away from Orchard Street for the next few days. I still didn't know about Mr. McCumber, but I knew that both he and Father wanted me to go see him. I told Helen, and she said that she understood and thought I was right, but I don't think she was really listening, because she was writing a letter to her pregnant daughter.

Finally, almost a week after the first visit, I decided to try and visit him. Just a short visit before lunch. So, I gathered my courage and marched the two blocks, determined not to back down. In truth, I was a little scared of Mr. McCumber. Nobody ever went to see him, except Father.

I knocked on the door, and almost immediately, it opened. This time, instead of easing open a crack, it swung wide open. This was a much more welcoming greeting already. "Hi," I said shyly.

"Hello, Katrina. How are you today?"

This was *much* nicer than a series of grunts like last time.

"I'm well, thank you. How are you?"

"All right. I'll be out in a second, I have something for you." He shut the door. I moved to the stool that I had used last time, wondering what on earth Mr. McCumber had for me.

When he reopened the door, I saw that he had a stack of books in his arms. "These are some that your father lent me. Would you mind returning them?" he asked.

Of course, he wanted me to bring back books. "Sure," I said.

"And there's one of mine that I thought you might like. It's called *Anne of Green Gables*, and it's more of a story fit for a little girl, and as I have none of those around . . ." he trailed off.

Then, he shook himself. "Tell me about yourself," he said.

"Well, I'm twelve years old, and my birthday is in September . . ."

I didn't realize that I could talk so much. He was such a good listener, and I told him everything. About school, and about Father, and what little I remembered of my mother.

When I finally stopped, he smiled. "Seems like you've had quite a full twelve years of it," he chuckled.

I was appalled. This man, who never spoke to anyone except Father, who really only grunted answers to Father, seemed like any other friendly man.

I nodded. Then Mr. McCumber stood up.

"How about some music?" he asked.

"That-that would be nice, if you don't mind."

"Oh, don't mind at all. Haven't had a real audience for a very long time, let alone a little girl to play for. Though you're not so little, about the age my Annelise . . ." he stopped, his face stricken.

Then he shook himself and went inside. He didn't emerge for a good five minutes, and I was beginning to get worried. I poked my head through the door, and there he was, his hand poised over the guitar, not moving.

"Mr. McCumber?" I asked.

He jerked and stared at me. "Who are you?" he asked.

"I'm Katrina Evans, Mr. Evans's

daughter, you were going to play for me."

"You're not Katrina. There's no Katrina. You're Annelise McCumber—don't try and fool me." He jerked again and shook his head. "Sorry Annelise . . . Katrina. My mind . . . it wanders." I was frightened, but I did my best not to show it.

"Yes, I understand." Though I didn't. "I-I think I'll be leaving now. It was nice to see you." My voice was about an octave higher than usual.

"Sure," Mr. McCumber grunted.

I turned and fled, forgetting the stack of books I had promised to bring home.

Chapter Four

Later, I told Father about what had happened.

"Mr. McCumber was right. His mind wanders," he said. "I am pretty sure that Annelise was the name of his daughter, the one who was your age when she died. I think he got the two of you confused," he explained.

"But why? I only talked to him this morning, and I've never *really* seen him before, except just on his porch. And I never saw her, but I doubt I look like his daughter, Annelise. Why would he get the two of us confused?" I demanded.

Father sighed.

"I don't know. I'm not a doctor nor a psychologist, but my best guess is this: You gave him a chance. You were nice to him. I know that all you did was go and see him, and on my urging, but I think that really meant a lot to him. I'm the only one that has gone to visit him in the three years he's lived here. And he knows that the main reason that I visit him is because it's a part of my work as the minister. I make calls to everyone, especially those who are in need. Not all ministers may say that is part of the job, but to me it is."

"Is there anything else we can do for him?" I asked.

"No, Kat. I think only he can do anything now. He has to learn to put his memories behind, and that is a very hard thing to do. I had a similar struggle after your mother died, but in a different fashion. I clung to anything and everything that was once hers. I tried to keep a slip of paper that she had written a grocery list on, thinking that maybe, if I had everything that she owned, it would be like she was still here. It was a good thing Helen came, and showed me that no matter what I held on to, it wouldn't bring her back. She helped me realize that the best thing I could do was care for you—make sure I held onto the things that you needed, not the little, silly things that I thought I needed."

I smiled and glanced up at Father.

"So should I go back today?"

He shook his head.

"Let him recover for a while and go back tomorrow. Maybe you two can talk about what happened today, if his mind is clearer."

I nodded. "Thanks, Father."

"Anytime."

I smiled at him, then went to find Helen.

She was in the kitchen, as usual, making lunch for Father and me.

"Anything I can do?" I asked.

"Nope, thanks. We have some leftovers from last night's dinner, some cold chicken and vegetables, so I'm just going to do that for lunch," she said.

"Alright."

Father said that I should wait to go and see Mr. McCumber, but I decided to just go pick up the books from his porch, then come back.

Mr. McCumber was inside his house. He had left the books on the porch. I picked them up, then turned away. Just as I was turning the corner, I looked back and saw Mr. McCumber's face peeking out the window. I smiled and continued around the corner.

I took Father's books to his study, then took the one for me, *Anne of Green Gables*, to my room. I sprawled out on my bed and opened the book.

Soon, I was lost in the story. I'm not sure how long I lay there, idly turning the faded brown pages, but soon Helen came and tapped me on the shoulder.

"What?" I asked,

"Come on, lunch is ready," she said.

I rolled off my bed and followed Helen into the kitchen. Father was sitting at the table, eating.

"Did you find a good book?" he asked with a smile.

"Oh, yes! Mr. McCumber gave it to me! It's about a girl. Her name is Anne, spelled with an 'e,' and she goes to live with a brother and sister, named Matthew and Marilla Cuthbert, except that they don't want her because she's not a boy."

"Sounds exciting."

I nodded, and sat down to eat my lunch.

Chapter Five

Over the next week, I visited Mr. McCumber four more times. Our visits usually ended with him confusing me with his daughter, Annelise, but I got used to him doing that, and stopped being scared when he did.

It turned out that Mr. McCumber was not the grumpy hermit I'd thought he was. He was only shy and chose to keep completely to himself. He reminded me of Matthew Cuthbert in *Anne of Green Gables*, who was also shy and timid. But Mr. McCumber didn't seem to mind me, or my chatter.

He played his guitar for me often. I had heard him of course, but the sound was much clearer than it was from my front porch.

In between these visits, I was preparing for the start of school. It was the end of August, and a new teacher was coming this year, so I was extra excited. Our town had so few children that there was only one teacher for everyone. The previous teacher, Mrs. Cotton, had been a strict woman, with iron grey hair and blue eyes that seemed to cut into you if you dared answer a question wrong. She was not that old, only forty, but she seemed as ancient as the soil. She had kept order only because no one dared cross her. Even the oldest pupils, who caused tons of trouble outside of school, were as well behaved as the smaller children, who were utterly terrified of her.

It was said that this new teacher was also a woman, but a young one, just out of school. She had grown up in Emerald Hills and gone off to college. I had never met her, but her name was Emily Ann White, and her father was the storekeeper.

Even if Miss White had no clue how to run a school, she would be better than Mrs. Cotton. One night, just before school started, I ran down to see Mr. McCumber. I had long ago finished *Anne of Green Gables*, but Mr. McCumber had provided more books about Anne, and I was reading the third one, *Anne of the Island*. The author, L.M. Montgomery, was a wonderful writer.

Anyway, I ran down to return *Anne of the Island*, which I had just finished. I knocked on his front door, and in a moment, it opened.

"Hi, Mr. McCumber!" I said breathlessly.

"Hey, what has you running over at this time?" he asked.

"I just wanted to return this book," I said, holding *Anne of the Island* out to him. "You are the most reliable person I know with books," he said with a laugh. "Why, if it was the middle of a blizzard, you would come here just to return a book."

I giggled. "Do you have any more books about Anne? I love them!"

"I don't, but I could get you one from the library. I have to go to town next week—got to fix a leak in my roof—and I'll get it then."

"Oh, Mr. McCumber! Thank you!" I threw my arms around his neck. He stiffened, and for a moment I was worried I had overstepped, that I shouldn't have hugged him, but after a moment he sort of patted my back and hugged me too.

After a second, I pulled away, and with a quick wave over my shoulder, I ran back home. Helen was in the kitchen, of course. Father was in his study, working. I decided to go to my loft.

My loft was in the barn. There was a tiny barn on the edge of our property, just a small, red structure that couldn't have held more than two horses. But it had a hay loft, and a few years ago, I had cleaned the loft out and made myself a small hideaway. There was a desk, and a large, slightly dusty couch, with some of the stuffing coming out. And I kept my small collection of books there, on a blue shelf.

There was a rag rug on the floor that was so thick it was quite comfortable to sit on. I chose a book and lay on my stomach on the center of the rug. Rain began to fall, but the loft was cozy and warm.

After a while, a loud ringing sound started. It was Helen, ringing the big iron bell outside the kitchen door. Whenever she rang it, I was to come quickly. Sometimes she rang it just because she had to ask me a little question, like "what do you want for lunch?" but usually she rang it because she needed me to do something.

So, I climbed down the ladder that led to the loft and ran across the field that separated the house from the barn. Helen was standing at the door, ringing the iron bell, earmuffs over her ears. I smiled. Helen said the bell was so loud that if she stood right next to it with her ears uncovered, she would surely lose her hearing. Still, it was funny to see her in the warm weather, wearing the puffy grey earmuffs that her son had got her.

When she saw me, she stopped

ringing and beckoned for me to come into the house. "I need your help with dinner," she said.

"What should I do?"

"Cut up the bread and set the table."

I did so while Helen bustled around making soup. In no time, we were sitting down to eat.

"Go get your father, hon. He's still working," Helen said.

I knocked on Father's door, and after a moment, it opened.

"Dinner's ready," I said.

"Alright. Be there in a second. I just have to finish this up," he said, gesturing to a pile of papers on his desk.

I turned back out of the room and went back to the kitchen.

"He's coming," I told Helen. Then I sat down at the table. Helen sat on one side of me, leaving the head of the table for Father. In a moment, I heard his soft footsteps come thudding through the hall and into the kitchen. He walked over to his chair and sat down.

Helen and I began to eat immediately, but Father did not. He put a hand to his chest and gulped a few deep breaths of air.

"Are you alright?" I asked through a mouthful of bread.

He smiled painfully.

"I'm alright," he promised. "And don't speak when your mouth is full of food," he added. The rest of the meal was silent, and as soon as it was over, Father retired to his room, murmuring about how he was "just a little tired, that's all."

Helen and I cleared the table, and she washed dishes while I put the extra soup away. "You know my daughter just had her baby?" Helen said suddenly.

"Oh! Helen! That's perfectly wonderful! Is it a boy or a girl? What's its name? When did she have him, her, it?" Babies were unfamiliar to me, as I had never really been around one.

"It's a little girl, and her name is Annie. She was born a week ago, but I just got the letter today." Helen was obviously hiding some important news. I could always tell, because she could not keep the excitement out of her voice, no matter how hard she tried.

"And she wants me to come and see her, with you and your father!" she burst out. "Oh! Oh!" was all I was able to say. Then, "*When?*"

"In two weeks, if your father can take time off of work."

"Oh!" I said again.

Helen's daughter lived in the big city, and while I had heard much about her, I had never actually met her. And now, on top of going to meet her, and going to see the city, I was going to see Helen's granddaughter!

I finished cleaning the kitchen with a new vigor and excitement, then went to tell Father the news.

He was very excited, but he seemed distracted, and not himself. So, I left him to his thoughts and went to get ready for bed.

Even though it was September, it was still sweltering in my bedroom. So I lay on the top of my blankets, sprawled over the entire surface of my bed. It was nice to lay there, in the heat. Everything felt slow and lazy; nobody was in a rush. The crickets and cicadas started up, and their noise was like a lullaby.

Chapter Six

I was happy. Not the kind of happy that comes crashing around your ears, but the kind that means everything is going great for you. It was a Saturday, and I had just gone to see Mr. McCumber. He had given me the next Anne of Green Gables book, called *Anne of Windy Poplars*. The book was tucked under my arm, along with another book from my friend Sara.

Sara was my age, and we were in the same class at school. But she lived just outside of town, "in the middle of nowhere" as she said. She had eight brothers and sisters, and her father worked in the city, building houses. She had a dozen chickens, two cows, and even a horse! She and her brother Michael rode the horse to school every day, since the walk was too long.

Sara had fascinated me, and I had fascinated her. That was what had first drawn us together, but now we were over our fascination and were just good friends.

I was walking from Mr. McCumber's house toward home. Tomorrow was Sunday, which usually would not have been a good thing, since Father was very strict and old-fashioned about Sundays, and I wasn't allowed to do any work or play. But this Sunday was going to be lots of fun because after church, there was going to be a party.

There wasn't any real reason for the party, except to have a good time. Also, it was the church's fifteen-year anniversary, so the party was sort of a celebration of that, I guess. I turned onto my street and broke into a run. Helen had probably been baking all day, and there would be lots of treats to sample: tarts, cookies, maybe even doughnuts. And maybe Helen wouldn't be done cooking and I could help her.

When I reached the house, I went into the kitchen. Helen was there, and so was Father. "Hey! How's Mr. McCumber?" Father asked.

"Good. Can I have something to eat?" I asked, spying the piles of pastries on the counter.

"No, Helen wants to eat dinner early so she can run into town afterwards. She has to get something for tomorrow. And besides, these are for the picnic, so we have to save them until tomorrow."

"What does she have to get?" I asked, grabbing a piece of bread from the pantry.

"I don't know, just some groceries. Now scoot. I have to get back to work."

I wandered into my room and opened the book Sara had lent me. It was a wonderful novel, full of adventure. And I was so lost in the story that it took Helen calling me three times to get my attention.

"What on earth are you doing in there?" she asked, exasperated.

"Sorry! I was in the middle of the most delightful book! See there was this little girl—"

"I don't need a rundown of the story. Just help me get dinner on the table. I have to go and get some ingredients. I'm making this fancy dessert for the picnic tomorrow. It's called a *Linzer torte*." Helen was careful with the pronunciation of the last word.

"Sorry!" I repeated. "What's a Linzer torte?"

"It's a fancy pastry with jam on the inside, and it's difficult. I need to make it tonight, because I can't do it before church, and your father would never ever hear of me missing church, even if I wanted to!" Helen said.

I helped her bring out dinner, and we sat down.

"Now where on earth is your father?" Helen muttered, standing back up again.

Father was where he always was, working.

"I swear, you'll work yourself to death one of these days!" Helen said, leading him to the table as if he were a small boy who had been naughty.

"I like my work though, and it's not like I'm doing manual labor all day," Father protested.

"Never mind that. Just eat," Helen instructed, sitting back down.

After dinner, Father and I cleaned the kitchen, while Helen gathered her hat and bag and flew off.

"Sometimes she reminds me of a bird, fluttering all over," Father remarked.

I laughed. "She does."

We went out on the porch, Father with a cup of coffee.

"Father, I was thinking," I said, a thought coming suddenly.

"Yes?"

"How exactly did Mr. McCumber's daughter die? I mean the one my age, who he gets me confused with. Annelise."

"I think," Father said slowly, "I think that she and her mother were in a train accident. They were killed in a fire that came from the engine and spread up the train."

"So you mean that his sons died in the war, and then he came back to find that his daughter and wife were dead?" I asked.

"Yes. Why?"

"I was just thinking . . . Mrs. Howard, whose going away party is tomorrow? She lost three sons in the war, almost as many as Mr. McCumber, and she's not as affected by grief. And, her husband died too!"

"Everyone copes with grief in different ways. Some clutch to things that must be let go, like the deceased's belongings. Some find new purposes in life that keep them going. Mrs. Howard adopted an orphan just after her husband died, and she was so focused on raising him that she could set aside her grief.

"Mr. McCumber had not had enough time to learn to cope with the grief he had after the death of his sons when he heard that the only other family he had left was dead. He's lost in his memories; that's another reason why he calls you Annelise."

"I think I understand," I said slowly.

"Good. But no more heavy talk now. While I *am* a minister, I'd like to put confusing topics such as grief to a rest and just enjoy this sunset."

I scooted closer to him and rested my head against his shoulder. We sat there until Helen came back, her arms full of packages. She went up the steps and into the kitchen, and I followed her.

"Helen, can I watch you make your fancy tart thing?" I asked.

"For now, but I'll bet that I'll still be working when it's time for you to go to bed. Your father wants you up bright and early, because he has to go and help decorate the church for the party and picnic afterwards. Why the minister has to help is beyond me. You'd think that the congregation could manage. But ah, well."

I smiled. Helen was not a fan of most of the congregation, even though she had been going to church with them for years. I sat down in my chair while Helen began unpacking her packages.

"Why did you buy jam when you had that lovely blueberry jam that would have been good?" I demanded when she pulled out two glass jars with pictures of raspberries on the tops.

"Because my recipe said to use raspberry jam, and there aren't raspberries ripe this time of year, and even if there were, I hate making jam. I make blueberry jam once a year to please your father, because it's his favorite, but I hate to make jam, so if I can, I'll buy it."

"Alright, there's no need to get angry," I said, slightly taken aback.

"Sorry. I'm tired, I guess, and stressed."

"Then why are you making the fancy tart thing?"

"Because I told Mrs. Howard that I would, and I intend to keep my word." Helen and Mrs. Howard, who owned a bakery, had a long-lasting rivalry about who could make the most complex desserts. Mrs. Howard had recently concocted a four-tier cake, but Helen refused to go to such extravagances and said that it wasn't fair because Mrs. Howard had an unlimited amount of ingredients while Helen could only buy a reasonable amount. She couldn't waste a dozen eggs and a full pound-and-a-half of flour on a fancy cake.

Chapter Seven

Around nine o'clock, I retired to my room. Helen's Linzer torte was in the oven, but she still had to wait for it to cool so that she could take it out of the pan, and I was tired. Father was in his study, and light peeked under the door, so I knew he was still awake. He often stayed up later on Saturday nights because he had to finish up his sermon. He always wrote it out before he gave it, because he said that if he didn't, he was apt to make a mistake, and then some person or other would say that he was not a suitable minister.

I pulled on my pajamas, and crawled into bed. Mr. McCumber was not playing his guitar, but the sounds of the night put me to sleep quickly.

The next morning I woke to my room filled with a wonderful orange-golden light. It was sunrise. I stretched and yawned, then rolled out of bed. I crept through the still-silent house to see if anyone else was awake.

Helen's beautiful Linzer torte sat on the table, all toasty and golden. Helen herself was not in the kitchen, so I peeked into her bedroom. She was sound asleep, her mouth slightly open.

There was a light coming from under Father's door, so I knocked softly. After a moment, the door opened. Father's hair was mussed, and there were dark circles under his eyes. "Oh, good morning, Katrina," he said distractedly.

"Good morning, Father. Are you okay?" I asked.

"Oh yes. Just fine." And he shut the door.

This was odd behavior for Father, but maybe he was just tired. I went into the kitchen to find myself some breakfast.

Two-and-a-half hours later, I was waiting for Father on the porch. I was dressed in my best dress, a pale-green one, and my hair was neatly braided. I held a basket full of flowers to decorate the church, and my shoes were shined so that I could see myself in them. Father came out carrying his notebook and wearing his best suit.

"Ready?" he asked.

"Yep!"

We walked down the front steps and started down the road.

By that time, I had forgotten Father's odd behavior earlier in the morning.

There were a few people at the church already, and I went over to one corner, where my friend Sara was arranging flowers in a vase.

"Hi, Sara!" I said.

"Hi, Katrina!" she said, turning to me with a smile.

"Did your whole family come?" I asked.

"Yep! Father took us in his car. He usually only uses it to get to work, and all eleven of us don't really fit, but we squeezed in so that we could all come. My younger brothers and sisters are around back, because they were causing utter chaos here," she said with a laugh. I laughed too and showed her the flowers I had brought.

"Could you use these?"

"Ooh! They're pretty! Go and see if my sister, Emma, can use them. I'm all full here. Emma's over there."

She pointed to a slim blonde girl standing on the other side of the church. I crossed over to Emma, and she took my flowers gratefully. Then I went to help Father hang garlands outside.

After a while, the rest of the congregation began to arrive. And one of the first ones was Helen, trotting up with her basket full of goodies. But there was something missing.

"Where's your Linzer torte?" I asked, peeking into the baskets to see if it was in there.

"I didn't want it to get ruined, so I'm just going to hop back and get it right as soon as church is over," Helen explained, with a glance at Mrs. Howard, who was coming up behind. I thought privately that the torte would not make an appearance at all if it was going to be outshone with another one of Mrs. Howard's four-tiered cakes.

Just then, Tommy, one of Sara's brothers, rang the big brass bell on the side of the church. This meant that the service would start any minute.

Helen set her baskets down and we found a seat next to Sara's family.

Everything went smoothly as we sang hymns and repeated prayers. Then, Father stepped into the pulpit.

"I would like us to start by repeating the Saint Francis prayer," Father said in his strong, clear voice.

The congregation said as one voice:

Lord, make me an instrument of your peace. Where there is hatred, let me sow love. Where there is injury, pardon. Where there is doubt, faith. Where there is despair, hope. Where there is darkness, light. And where there is sadness, joy.

"Oh, divine master, grant that I may not so much seek to be consoled as to console—"

I didn't hear the rest, because there was something wrong with the man in the pulpit. He looked up, as if there was something of great interest on the ceiling. His hand clutched at his chest, and then his eyes locked with my own.

Something changed just then. The eyes I had known my entire life, the eyes that had seemed to have candles lit in them, bringing warmth and happiness to all around, changed. I can't tell you exactly how they changed, but the best way I can explain is this. The candles that had shown all his life, went out.

Chapter Eight

I don't think anyone else saw it until the last line of the prayer had been uttered—". . . and it is in dying that we are born to eternal life."

Then someone screamed. I don't know who. It might have been me.

Because the man in the pulpit had crumpled and was lying on a heap on the floor. A man rushed up. It was Doctor Cunningham.

My heart was pounding against my ribs, as though it thought that if it beat faster and harder, it would make the man in the pulpit's heart not be through beating. The doctor stood

Sara was on one side of me, and I then became aware that she was clutching my hand, and I don't know whose hand it was, or if it was both of us who had such sweaty hands.

back up again, his face grim.

"There's nothing we can do for him," he said.

The walls were closing in.

I was hot, even though it was a cool day.

Sara was talking to me. What was she saying? It didn't matter.

There was a rushing in my head.

And everything went black.

———————————————————

I woke to someone wiping my forehead with a cool cloth. I was lying down, and above me, I could see the underside of the church roof. Helen's face swam into view. "Katrina, are you awake?" she asked softly.

I moaned and nodded my head slightly.

Helen disappeared, and I turned my head to keep her in focus. Sara was on one side of me, and I then became aware that she was clutching my hand, and I don't know whose hand it was, or if it was both of us who had such sweaty hands.

Then I turned toward the pulpit. No one was there.

"Where's—" I started. Then I remembered.

"They moved your father's body a few minutes ago, darling," said another woman, Sara's mother.

"His body?" I asked. "There's nothing they could do to save him?"

Tears filled Helen's eyes as she shook her head. I rolled over, and realized that I was lying on the floor, which was not at all comfortable.

I didn't care.

Tears didn't come. I wanted them to. I felt that my father deserved all the tears I could shed, but they wouldn't come.

"Go get that McCumber man— he's Katrina's good friend," someone said. My eyes were screwed tight, but I thought it might have been Mrs. Howard.

Sara withdrew her hand, and I heard her leave the church. I rolled over back onto my back, and sat up.

"I don't need any help. I am perfectly okay," I said in a voice that was not my own. I pulled myself up and walked carefully to the door. Sara was outside, walking quickly. I ran to catch up with her, but soon found that that was a bad idea. My head started to spin again. "Sa-ara!" I yelled. "Come ba-ack!" She turned, and saw that it was me yelling. She did turn, and came at me at top speed, crashing into me.

"Oh! Katrina! I'm so sorry!" she cried, her tears wetting my shoulder. "I'm sure Mother and Father will let you live with us if you want! Is there anything I can do for you?"

"No, I'm okay. I just want to walk, that's all." My voice was still not my own.

"Oh . . . alright." She stepped back, and I walked past her.

Maybe that was rude, but I didn't care. I just had to be alone. I walked, not exactly sure where I was going. But, I found myself home, in my father's study. I walked over to his desk and saw an envelope, and there was a name written on the envelope. My name.

I picked up the envelope and opened it with Father's letter opener. Then I sank into Father's bed and began to read the words carefully written in his neat script.

My dearest Katrina,

Although I know that it probably will not, I hope this letter finds you in good spirits. I know that it is difficult to lose a parent. My own mother died when I was ten. But I also know that you are a strong, brave girl who will push through and not let her grief swallow her.

Even if you suffer, you will go on in life and find other things to be happy about. You will love, and laugh, and be happy. And that's exactly what I want for you. Like I said, I know how hard it is to lose someone, but life does go on. And if you don't let it go on, then it will pile up and come crashing down on you when you least want it.

I have always had a weak heart. They didn't think I would live when I was a baby. I am giving this letter to Helen, who also knows of my weak heart, and she will give it to you. She will care for you for a little while, but you must go to someone who can take care of you forever.

Helen is old, but not too old. Still, she's not the age to bring up a child, even a child as good and intelligent as you.

Know that I wish all the best for you,
Father

I was crying then. So he had known that he might die, and he had not warned me or prepared me. But I was too worn out and tired to be angry, so I clutched the letter to my chest and fell back onto Father's bed, letting my tears fall thick and fast.

Helen came in later and told me what was to be done. There would be a small funeral next week, and we would sell this house. It was Helen's house now; Father had left it to her, but she couldn't keep it. And besides, she wanted to be nearer to her daughter.

She and I would move to the city to stay with her daughter until we could find a place of our own. Then, we would try and find me another home with someone who could care for me. I barely registered a word.

Chapter Nine

The next three days were a blur. Sara visited often, but left quickly. I knew that it was because I was being unsociable, but I couldn't help it. I read Father's letter every day, and it helped to ease some of the pain, but not much.

I helped Helen pack up our belongings, and slowly, the house transformed from the home it had been all my life to an empty skeleton of a place, filled only with memories. On Wednesday, I had another visitor: Mr. McCumber. He came bursting into my room, where I was packing my clothes into a bag.

"Stop," he ordered.

I looked up, surprised, and replaced the dress I was holding into the closet. "No, not packing. Well, do stop for a moment. I need to have a serious talk with you." I had never seen him this stern. I walked over and sat on my bed. He sat down heavily next to me.

"You need to stop," he said. "You're going the same way I went. You're getting lost. Soon you won't know yourself, and you'll realize that you've pushed everyone who loves you away. You need to stop and put your grief behind you. You need to focus on what comes next, and what you need to do for Helen, and for Sara, and all the other people that you care about. You need to do what your father would expect of you!"

I was astonished. Never had he been so opinionated and sure of himself. No longer was he the man who got me confused with his own dead daughter, or lost himself to his sad memories. I felt a lump rise in my throat, and tears formed in my eyes. I squeezed them back, but it was no use. Mr. McCumber put an arm around me, and held me, letting me soak his shirt with my tears.

When my sobs subsided, he pulled back to look me in the eye.

"Are you finished?"

I nodded, and he hugged me again.

From then on, things did get better. The funeral was heart-wrenching, but it did not send me back into the state I'd been in for the first three days.

Afterward, I helped Helen pack our things into a large truck from the city, and then we were driven to Helen's daughter's house. We had lots of help unpacking, and then that was that. I no longer lived in Emerald Hills. Helen's daughter, Madeline, was lovely. And her baby, Annie, was so chubby and she smiled all the time. I

slept in a tiny room that used to be a closet, because there weren't enough bedrooms. But it was a large closet, large enough to have a bed, so I was content enough.

I kept to myself mostly. There was a library down the street, and I would curl up with a good book and read for hours. Helen cooked enough food to feed the entire city, but her daughter did not seem to mind; she just laughed and told Helen not to fill up all of her kitchen, because if she kept baking and baking, there would soon be so much food that no one could get into the kitchen.

Baby Annie was too little to do anything, and it seemed that all of Madeline's time was spent caring for her. Even when Annie was sleeping, Madeline was stitching a dress for her, or knitting a sweater, or doing her laundry.

Another thing that I did a lot of was write. I was not one for writing stories, but I wrote enough letters to fill a book. I wrote to Sara, and Mr. McCumber mostly, but I also wrote to some of my other friends, like Emily Ann, who I didn't see often because her parents went to a church in the city and she was sent to a private school in the city. I wondered if I would see Emily Ann now that I was in the city, and I asked her where her school was, but it was on the other side of the city.

One night, Helen came into my bedroom. I knew why she was there. I had been waiting for her to come for a while.

"Look, Katrina . . ." she started slowly.

"No, I know why you're here. I can't

stay here and we need to find a place for me to live. I understand," I said quickly.

"Oh, good," said Helen uncomfortably.

"I have no idea what to do though, if you were wondering. I could go back to Emerald Hills, maybe live with Sara?" I suggested.

Helen looked even more uncomfortable. "I actually wrote Sara's parents a couple of weeks ago. They said that they were very sorry, but they just couldn't take you, because Sara's mother is expecting another baby, and they couldn't really add one more."

"Alright. Then send me to a boarding school. I'll work on the weekends to earn my keep."

"I already thought of that too, but all the boarding schools are too expensive . . . And besides, I might as well send you to an orphanage."

"Then why don't you?"

"Because there are no suitable ones. They are all poor, and I haven't found one where the matron was a woman who knew anything about children."

"Then I'll help you look. There's nothing else to be done."

I wanted to be off of Helen's hands as much as she did. I did not like living at the expense of others, and I knew that Madeline and her husband wanted me out of the house, especially with the new baby and all.

Chapter Ten

A week later, I was moving again. Helen had found an orphanage that was not as poor as the others, and the matron was a young, caring woman. So, I repacked my belongings, and Madeleine's husband drove me over one Monday morning before he went to work.

The orphanage was an intimidating brick building that stretched high up into the sky. There was an iron archway before the door, with vines growing up both sides. Madeline's husband knocked on the door, and a moment later, it opened to reveal a rosy-faced girl of about fourteen, wearing a blue dress with a white apron overtop. "Hello, I am Richard Cooper. May I please speak to Miss Rebecca Smith?" Mr. Cooper asked.

"Yessir. Come in and I'll go get her, sir," said the girl, opening the door wider. We stepped into a dimly lit hall with blue and green braided rugs positioned at different intervals across the floor.

The girl who had let us in climbed the huge set of stairs at the other side of the room and disappeared behind a large oak door.

A moment later she reappeared, followed by a woman who must have been Miss Smith.

She was very short and stout, with cheeks even rosier than the other girl. She had pretty black hair that was pulled back in a bun. Little wisps of hair fell into her face, and she brushed them aside with a pudgy finger.

"Well!" she said when her eyes fell upon Mr. Cooper and me. "I'm delighted to see you. I know who you are, Mr. Cooper, but I guess that you," looking at me, "are Katrina Evans."

"Yes ma'am," I said quietly.

"I am Miss Rebecca Smith, and this

here," she gestured to the girl who had let us in, "is Mary Rogerson. She helps me here because there are far too many girls for me to take care of all alone. It's such a pity. There are four orphanages in the city, and all of them are filled to bursting. Mine is the least full, but that is because we have less room than the other three."

As Miss Smith spoke, she led us upstairs and into the room that Mary Rogerson had entered to fetch her. It was an office with a desk and chair, a fat leather couch, and two large bookcases.

"Now," said Miss Smith, sitting down on the chair. "Make yourselves at home, and we'll get everything all settled."

I sat down on the edge of the leather couch, not sure I wanted to make myself at home here quite yet.

"Mary, would you please take Miss Evans to her dormitory? I think that might be better than just sitting here," suggested Miss Smith. Mary nodded, and beckoned for me to follow her out the door.

"Am I going to share a room with the other girls?" I asked. "And where are the other girls?" as an afterthought.

"To answer your first question, yes. You'll share a room with three other girls. We don't have half enough rooms for all the girls to get their own. And to answer your second question, the girls are in the schoolrooms downstairs, learning their lessons. My sisters, Amelia and Peggy, teach the lessons," explained Mary.

"Do you have any other sisters?" I asked. "Or brothers?"

Mary chuckled. "Too many of them. There's twelve of us all together. Amelia's the oldest, then Peggy, then me. My brother, he comes right after me. He works at the store a couple of blocks away. We all have to work to help Mother and Father out. My next sister, Anne, is just about your age, so she's still home to help with the really young ones," she explained.

We were standing in front of a door with a piece of paper tacked to it. On the paper were four names: Olivia Winslow, Abigail Hayes, Natalie Gardiner, and Katrina Evans. Mary opened the door and stepped inside. There were two bunk beds, one on each side of the room. There was another braided rug, like the ones downstairs, in the center of the floor. There were two large closets against the back wall, and two desks on either side of the door. Mary led me to a bunk on the right-hand side of the room.

"You get the bottom bunk, since Abigail already has the top. Natalie and Olivia sleep on the other side," she explained.

I nodded mutely and set my bag down on my bunk.

"You are excused from the first lesson this morning, since you've just arrived and all, but you'll take part in the next one that begins in half an hour. You get yourself comfortable, and I'll come fetch you when it's time." Then, she swept out of the room.

Moments later, she poked her head back in. "The desk farther from the wall is yours, and you can fill half of the closet on the right side of the room," she told me, then withdrew her head.

I sat down on my bed and stared

around the room. This was where I would live, probably until I was cightccn and old cnough to carc for myself. So for five years.

But, there was no use in moping. I opened my bag and began to unpack my clothes into one half of the dresser. It seemed that the girl whom I shared the closet with, Abigail Hayes, was not very neat, but let her things get strewn all over the closet. I pushed her things to one side, and placed my clothes on the shelves neatly.

I hung up my dresses, then put my books into my desk. I put Father's letter, the one he had written just before he died, under my pillow. Then, I shoved my bag under my bed and laid down on top of my bed.

After a while, Mary reappeared, and told me to come with her; it was time for lessons. "You'll be with my closest sister, Peggy. She's real sharp, and nothing gets past her, so don't try to misbehave in her class. You'll sit with your roommates, Olivia, Natalie, and Abigail," Mary said.

She led me to a door and knocked lightly. A young woman opened it. She was the spitting image of her sister, with the same rosy cheeks and wide smile. She had the same dark curls as Mary, and the same laughing eyes.

"Hello! You must be Katrina. I'm Peggy Rogerson," said the young woman. I smiled shyly. She led me through the door and over to a group of four desks. Three of the desks were filled, but the fourth was vacant.

"Girls, this is Katrina Evans, your new roommate. Katrina, this is Olivia, Natalie, and Abigail. Why don't you all gct to know cach other? Wc havc a few more minutes before we need to start," said Peggy, then she went up to the large desk at the front of the room.

I sat down slowly, aware that all three girls were looking at me. Olivia sat to my right. She was tall and thin, with long blonde curls that fell past her waist.

Natalie sat across from me. She was very skinny, but not underfed. She had long arms and legs, and a great deal of freckles. She had bright green eyes, and short little waves of thick red hair.

The last girl, who sat to my left, was Abigail, whom I shared a bunk and closet with. She was even taller than Olivia, and she had dark brown hair that was pulled into a long plait down her back. She had dark eyes, and when she smiled, small dimples appeared in both her cheeks. "Hi," I said quietly.

"Hi! I'm Natalie Gardiner, and I'm eleven. How old are you?" asked Natalie. She had a bubbly, loud voice, and seemed not at all shy.

"Thirteen," I replied.

"Abbey's thirteen too!" Natalie said. "And Olivia is twelve," she added.

"Don't call me Abbey," ordered Abigail. Her dimples were not there, and she was looking right at Natalie.

Natalie did not cower under the older girl's stare; she just giggled.

"You're so touchy about being called Abbey, but why? It's not a bad name," she said.

"It's none of your business," muttered Abigail.

I made a mental note never to call her Abbey.

Olivia, who had not spoken yet, asked, "Did both your parents die? My mother did, when I was born. My father was away at sea, and he's still in Ireland. He keeps saying how he's going to come back, but it's been twelve years."

"Yes, my mother died when I was a toddler, and my father died two months ago," I said.

"I don't know what happened to my parents," remarked Natalie. "I've been here all my life, and nobody has any record of who my parents were."

I didn't get to ask any more questions because just then, Peggy Rogerson called from the front of the room, "Alright, everyone! Open your books to page 112. We're going to start with decimals."

Abigail handed me a math book, and I flipped through it to page 112.

Chapter Eleven

Even if you think you'll never ever get used to something, if you do it long enough, you do. I'll bet that someone could get used to anything.

Well, when I moved in, I thought that I would hate everything about life there. I thought I would hate the matron, Miss Smith. I thought I would hate the girls and the food, everything.

But I found myself slowly growing accustomed to life in the orphanage. I liked Olivia and Abigail and Natalie, and I liked my lessons. I was learning more than I had been back in Emerald Hills. The food was delicious, almost as good as Helen's, and I had three square meals a day.

One morning, I woke up to find that I had burrowed deep into my bed. Only the top of my face was sticking out from the covers, and it was icy. I opened my eyes, and saw that there were two mounds of blankets on the bunks across from me. From one lump protruded a red-haired head, and from the other, great masses of golden hair. I was sure that if I could see through Abigail's mattress, she too would be curled up underneath the blankets. I took a deep breath and threw the covers off. I immediately wanted to throw them back on, but I didn't. I pulled socks on over my bare feet, and wrapped my quilt around me, since my light cotton nightgown was not thick enough to keep me warm.

I tiptoed across the room and opened my closet. I put on my warmest dress (Miss Smith did not approve of girls in pants) and a thick sweater. I pulled my hair into two braids, then returned my quilt to my bed. I was usually the first to rise out of my roommates, and I liked to sneak downstairs and go out onto the back porch to watch the sunrise. Today, I grabbed a thick coat from the closet in the hall.

The back door was open, and I heard voices coming from outside. I knew it was impolite to listen, but the people who were speaking were speaking so quietly that I couldn't make out the words. But then, the voices grew louder, and I heard a voice that sounded like Miss Smith's say, "No, I can't! The children—" then another voice that sounded like a man's said, "Get someone else to take over. You've been at this job for ten years, and you can be done."

Then, Miss Smith gave a loud sigh, and said, "Alright. I'll get someone. Give me a month, and then I'll be ready to announce it."

I decided that this was enough. I wasn't going to spy on Miss Smith any longer. I pushed the back door open and stepped out, blinking in the first bright rays of sunlight. Miss Smith was sitting beside a tall, dark-haired man. When she saw me, she gasped and stood up quickly.

"Oh my, Katrina. Did you hear . . .? Never mind. This is my friend, Mr. Charles Elliot. Charlie, this is one of the children, Katrina Evans," she said.

"Do you know that it's bad manners to come bursting in on someone like that?" Mr. Elliot asked coldly.

"I'm sorry—" I started, but Miss Smith cut me off.

"Charlie, she didn't know we were out here. You don't usually come in the mornings, and Katrina often comes out here to watch the sunrise."

"Well, as long as it doesn't happen again," muttered Mr. Elliot. Then, under his breath, so that I could hardly hear, I heard him whisper to Miss Smith, "Not that it will." Miss Smith blushed.

"Well, I'm going to walk Mr. Elliot out. Enjoy the sunrise!" she said to me. They left around the side of the building, and I settled into a chair, pondering. What was this? Who really was Mr. Charles Elliot? And what was Miss Smith saying about getting someone to take over?

Someone to take over the orphanage? But what if the new woman was not as kind and gentle as Miss Smith? What if she was mean and unfeeling?

I shook myself and focused on the sun, which was just coming up between tall buildings of the city.

Chapter Twelve

At breakfast, I told my roommates what I had witnessed.

"Maybe she's going to marry Mr. Elliot," suggested Natalie.

"But then she would leave us!" said Olivia.

"She did say that she was going to get someone to take her place," I reminded them.

"But maybe she meant something else. Maybe she's the leader of some secret society, and she has to step down!" said Natalie excitedly.

"Don't be ridiculous," said Olivia.

"I don't know, but I think Natalie's right," Abigail said thoughtfully.

"About being a leader of a secret society?" I asked.

"No, about Miss Smith getting married. I wouldn't be surprised."

"Wanna bet?" Natalie asked.

"No! Natalie!" Olivia said incredulously.

I laughed. Even though Olivia and Natalie were only a year apart, their relationship was very much like an older sister and a much younger sister.

Just then, Miss Smith stepped up onto the platform at the front of the dining room. "Girls, I have an announcement to make. It will probably come as a surprise, and I am sure you will have your questions, but

I ask that you let me finish before you ask them.

"I am a young woman, much like yourselves, although I am much older than all of you. And, although plenty choose not to, most women marry. And, my news is that I am engaged to someone—Mr. Charles Elliot!

"I know this will come as a shock. And like I said, I know you have questions, and I am happy to answer them now.

"We are going to be married in six months' time, in June. We are going to stay in the city, but an orphanage is not a very good home for a just-married couple. So, the sad news is that I will be leaving you all.

"And, I am not leaving today, nor am I leaving at the end of the six months. I am going to interview anyone who would like to take my position, and when I find someone who will take proper, good care of you, then I will step down and he or she will step up."

She looked around the hall at all of our blank faces. Then, a little girl of about seven, stood up.

"Are you going to come back?" she asked.

Miss Smith smiled. "No, child. I am not. That is, not for a while. I don't know what life holds for me, but I think that I will not be back before you are gone from this place." Nobody else had any questions, so Miss Smith directed us to finish our meals and then clean up for morning lessons.

As soon as she sat back down, a buzz of conversation rippled around the hall. "Told you!" crowed Natalie. "I knew she was going to be married! I just knew it!"

"But what if the new matron is not nice at all?" Olivia asked worriedly.

"Miss Smith won't let that happen," Abigail said confidently.

After breakfast, we went into Amelia Rogerson's classroom. I liked Peggy better than her older sister because Peggy let us do things, like build tiny catapults and learn about plants with real samples of the plant. Amelia, however, had us read everything from books. We read our lessons, recited passages sometimes, and wrote our sums neatly for her to look over. We all filed to our desks, and sat down. I sat with Abigail because we shared a bunk, while Olivia and Natalie sat together in front of us.

Abigail was a bit of a mystery to me. She was very quiet, and hardly said anything. She was very bright, and hardly ever made mistakes in school. But she seemed more comfortable with her schoolbooks than with people.

Mr. McCumber had given me a full set of the *Anne of Green Gables* books before I'd left Emerald Hills, and I had let Olivia and Natalie read them, and they had loved them just as much as I did. But Abigail just smiled, and said that they were good little stories, but she should really get back to her work.

I also did not know where Abigail was from. Natalie had told me that she had no idea where her parents were from, or who they were exactly, just that they had both died when she was too little to remember, and their names were Hannah and Carl Gardiner. Olivia's mother had died, and her father was in Ireland, but I had absolutely no idea about Abigail; I didn't even know if she knew where her parents were from, or who they were. Maybe she was like Natalie with no clues. But Natalie knew names, and surely Abigail knew her parents' names. But maybe she just didn't like to talk about it. I knew that I didn't. I had told Olivia and Natalie because they'd asked, but it seemed that they could have begged Abigail on bended knee and she would not have given a word.

Amelia was having us do a grammar lesson, which was boring even when Peggy taught it. The morning dragged on and on, and when the bell rang signaling the end of the first lesson, I couldn't have been more relieved.

For lunch, the cook had a big cart filled with brown bags. Today, each girl was to take a bag and go eat in their room. They were not to make a mess. Usually, we would eat in the dining room, but today, Miss Smith was interviewing a possible matron. Miss Smith wanted to be able to talk over lunch in peace in the dining room, so she asked that the girls eat in their rooms.

Abigail, Olivia, Natalie, and I sat in a circle on the floor to eat. There were sandwiches for lunch, as well as an apple for each girl, and a cookie.

After we had finished, we disposed of our bags and went back to Peggy's classroom for our afternoon lesson. However, when we got there, Peggy was closing the door. "Sorry, ladies. We won't have lessons this afternoon. Miss

Smith has already hired a new matron. I think she's rushing into it, but I'm sure she wants to wash her hands of this job. It's not my place to criticize her, so I'll just tell you that you're supposed to go to the dining hall so that Miss Smith can introduce you."

We turned back around and walked with Peggy into the dining hall. We took our places at our table and looked expectantly with the rest of the girls at the platform. Miss Smith was standing there, alongside a woman who reminded me greatly of Marilla Cuthbert from *Anne of Green Gables*. She was tall and thin, with pinched features and iron-colored hair pulled back in a bun so tight that it looked like it was stretching the skin on her face. She had long, bony fingers, and her eyes were black.

"Girls," Miss Smith said. "I am so pleased to announce that I have already found a suitable matron for you. This is Miss Malcolm, and I expect you to be courteous and respectful to her."

"I will not tolerate rulebreakers," Miss Malcolm said in a booming voice. "Those who believe that rules are above them are the ones who will suffer. However, if you abide by my rules, a few of which will be different than they were under Miss Smith, then you will be perfectly happy and comfortable."

Everyone stared up at her with blank faces. This was going to be our new matron? What was this going to be like . . . ? I had a horrible flashback to another one of the orphanages that Helen and I had visited. The matron there looked very similar to this woman, except her name was Mrs.

West. She had ruled her orphans with a rod of iron, and the children there were miserable—I had seen it in their eyes.

How was this new appointment going to change life at the orphanage where I had learned to live happily?

Chapter Thirteen

Life was very different, and not in a good way. Miss Smith departed the following day, and Miss Malcolm moved in.

Miss Smith always made sure that there was enough room for everyone to be comfortable before she took more orphans, but Miss Malcolm took four more orphans in one day! Also, on the first day, Natalie and Olivia got on her bad side. I'm not exactly sure what happened, but I could hear Miss Malcolm yelling about how they were a disgrace.

So, when the four orphans moved in (even though all the rooms were full), they were all put in our room. Olivia and Natalie apologized profusely, saying that it was all their fault, and I assured them it wasn't, and that they were forgiven. All Abigail said was, "It's only *her* fault. She shouldn't have taken the orphans anyway; we don't have room. And she did it to punish all of us. I heard her telling the milkman this morning that she hates children, and only took this job because it pays well."

"So we're stuck with a lady who doesn't even like us because Miss Smith was in a rush to get married," I summed up.

"Yep," sighed Olivia.

We walked up the stairs to our dormitory. We went in and were

appalled by what we saw.

"They're . . ." I started.

". . . babies," finished Natalie.

The room that had once held two bunks and four desks now held one bunk, two desks, two cribs, and a changing table.

"I thought that there was another section of the orphanage for babies!"

"There is," Abigail said darkly.

"Then why . . . " My question was answered in a second as Miss Malcolm came swooping in.

"Oh! Lovely. You're here. We have four more orphans coming to us today. They're from my sister, Mrs. West's orphanage. She had *far* too many. And I know that it's not usual procedure, but the upper floors where the youngest children live are stuffed full. So, I thought that you four might like to care for these little ones!" She sounded like she was telling us we had just won some grand prize.

"You're now sharing your room with Rosemary, Sophia, Penelope, and Ruby." Four girls toddled in. The oldest looked about four, and the youngest about two. They walked holding each other's hands, and each was dirtier than the last.

"Good! Now you can get to know each other. I expect all eight of you to be clean before dinner!" Miss Malcolm said as she swept back out of the room.

Rosemary, who was the oldest looking, went and sat down on the bottom bunk.

"How old are you?" Natalie asked Rosemary.

Rosemary said nothing, but held up four fingers.

"What about the rest of you?"

Natalie asked, turning to them.

Two of the girls were exactly identical, and one of them spoke up.

"I am Penny. My full name is Penelo—I can't say it. I'm this many!" She held up three fingers.

Rosemary, who seemed to be the leader of the little group, spoke then.

"Penny and me have long names, so we like to use short names. I am Rose. And Penny is Penny. Ruby and Sophia have short names. Penny and Ruby have the same birthday! They are twins. Sophia is two. She doesn't talk."

"Alright," said Olivia slowly. "I am Olivia. This is Natalie, Abigail, and Katrina." she pointed to each of us. "We are going to take care of you. Do you want to get cleaned up?"

One of the twins, I'm not sure whether it was Ruby or Penny, nodded. We each took one of the younger girls' hands and led them to the washroom.

By this time, I was used to change and getting used to things. I got used to the fact that Miss Malcolm did not like me or any of my friends. I got used to waking up in the middle of the night to soothe the frightening dreams of the little girls. I got used to helping with four baths every night, along with my own. I got used to helping someone eat every bite of every meal.

After a few days, Abigail, Natalie, Olivia, and I had a meeting after lights out. That was much easier than it used to be, because we were all sleeping in one bunk bed. Abigail and I shared the bottom bunk, and Olivia and Natalie slept above us.

"We have to do something! This is not fair. We're late to our lessons,

we're late to meals. We're not these girls' mothers!" Natalie whispered angrily.

"There's nothing we can do. Miss Malcolm is in charge, and if we cross her, we'll be worse off than we are now," I said.

"So we just have to keep going? This is miserable!" Natalie said.

"I guess so."

"I know what will make it easier, though," Abigail said. "We each take charge of one girl. That way all the work is divided, and we're not all trying to do everything."

"That would be better," agreed Olivia.

"Why doesn't Natalie be in charge of Rose, since Natalie's the youngest and Rose needs the least attention?" suggested Abigail.

"Okay," agreed Natalie.

"Would it be alright if I'm in charge of Sophia?" Olivia asked.

"Sure. Then Katrina and I can be in charge of the twins," said Abigail.

"We'd better go back to our bed," I said nervously.

Abigail climbed down with me and we snuggled down into the covers. Now, in the cold, it was nice to have the extra body heat, but I was not looking forward to the summer, when the bed would feel far too hot and small for two half-grown girls.

Chapter Fourteen

This new idea did work well. Abigail and I shared charge of the twins because they refused to be separated. And it was easier to get to things on time when there were half the amount of girls to take care of. And Olivia and

I was about to speak up when Abigail did. Abigail, who I had never heard raise her voice, or even speak very much at a time, shouted loud enough to rival Miss Malcolm.

Natalie seemed to like the new system too. But I should have known it was too good to last.

About two weeks after the girls came, we were in lessons when Miss Malcolm started to yell.

"Katrina Evans! Natalie Gardiner! Olivia Winslow! Abigail Hayes! Your roommates . . . Get into my office!" she yelled.

We leaped from our desks, and Peggy didn't try to stop us. She knew that when Miss Malcolm yelled like that, you'd better listen.

The four of us ran into Miss Malcolm's office to see four flour-covered figures standing just inside the doorway.

"You—you left these girls unsupervised, and they got into the kitchen and practically bathed in the flour. That was sixty pounds of flour that I had just bought for Cook that is now ruined! What do you have to say for yourselves?" she demanded.

"We were in our lessons, ma'am. We told them to stay in our room, but I guess they didn't listen."

"You're right! Well, they did not listen!" shouted Miss Malcolm. "I need you to take care of these girls because I already have too much to do! If that means that you must miss your lessons, then miss them!"

This was the most unfair statement I had ever heard. I was about to speak up when Abigail did. Abigail, who I had never heard raise her voice, or even speak very much at a time, shouted loud enough to rival Miss

Malcolm.

"Do you know what it's like to live in an orphanage? No! Do you know what it's like to have your parents leave you at that orphanage because they don't want you? No! Do you know what it is like to have four toddlers pushed upon you because the person who cares for them cannot be bothered by them? Do you know what it is like to spend every waking minute worrying because one of those toddlers might get into trouble or get sick? No! You don't! And that is why I'm leaving. You can take your toddlers back, and care for them like you said you would!"

Abigail turned and stormed out of the room.

Miss Malcolm was stunned into silence. So was I. So was Olivia. So was Natalie. The only people not stunned were the four flour-covered little girls.

Miss Malcolm recovered first.

"Out! Get these girls cleaned up! I will not hear another word, not one more word!" she said.

Olivia, Natalie, and I gathered the little girls and herded them out the door. The girls were silent as we bathed them and gave them fresh clothes. Perhaps they thought that their naughtiness was what had caused Abigail to leave.

It was something else, though.

I couldn't talk to Natalie and Olivia until nightfall, when we were all supposed to be asleep. After sleeping with Abigail, the bed felt big and empty. I remembered how I used to dread summer coming because we would be so squished. Now, I would give anything to have my bedmate back.

I climbed the ladder and sat at the foot of the bed.

"Did you know?" I whispered.

"No," both girls said together.

"No wonder Abigail didn't want to talk about her family," murmured Olivia.

"They just left her?" asked Natalie.

"That's what it sounds like," I told her.

"Do you think she's gone for good?" Natalie asked.

Olivia and I looked at each other.

"We don't know," Olivia said.

Just then, there was a knock on our door. I scrambled down the ladder and jumped into my bed. Once I was there, I called in a pretend sleepy voice, "Come in."

The door eased open, and a head poked in. It wasn't Miss Malcolm.

It was Abigail.

Chapter Fifteen

"Abigail?" I asked.

"Good. You're awake," she said as a way of greeting. "I need your help."

"What with?" Olivia asked.

"I need to get my things. I'm running away. Also, I came to see if any of you wanted to come with me. I'm going to take the twins. That way they'll be off your hands. I was just going to take Penny, but Ruby would die if they were separated, so I have to take them both."

"I'm coming!" Natalie said immediately.

"Olivia? Katrina?" Abigail asked.

"I'd love to, but, oh! If Miss Malcolm

got us, we'd be dead!" Olivia cried.

"Shh! You'll wake the little ones. Katrina?" Abigail turned toward me.

I was fighting a battle against myself. If I went, then I would be an outcast, no longer a good part of society. Would Father be ashamed of me? Or would he be ashamed because I was letting Miss Malcolm boss me and treat me unfairly?

"I'm going."

"Great. Are you sure you don't want to, Olivia?" Abigail asked.

"Oh, I guess, if you are all going!" Olivia said, climbing down the ladder.

We packed all of our belongings that we could, leaving the unimportant things. Then, we each put the small items that belonged to the younger girls into our bags. We each picked up a sleeping child, then stole downstairs.

Ruby stayed fast asleep in my arms. She looked like a little angel, her golden curls fanned out around her chubby face. She did not at all look like a girl who just earlier that day had decided to play in a sixty-pound bag of flour.

Somehow, we got out of the orphanage without Miss Malcolm, any of the other orphans, or any of the Rogerson sisters seeing us.

We crept down the dark street, giggling with excitement.

"Where should we go?" Natalie asked.

"We can stay the night at my aunt's," Abigail said. "She doesn't know I was at an orphanage, but she lives close by. She has five children, and can't keep us, but she could for just one night. I know that."

We agreed and followed Abigail

down another street.

The sleeping girls were getting heavier by the minute, and our bags weren't getting any lighter. We stopped often, and each time we stopped for longer. But finally, we made it to Abigail's aunt's house.

Abigail gently set Penny down on the porch swing and knocked on the door. After a moment it opened to reveal a tall, slim woman. She had the same dark hair as Abigail, and a similar face.

"Abbey? Is that you? I haven't seen you in ever so long! Where are your parents? And who is your . . . entourage?" the woman said.

"I'm so sorry, Aunt Claire. I can explain in a second, but do you have a bed where we can put the girls?" Abigail asked.

"Yes, come and put them up in the spare bed. But Abbey where—" Aunt Claire opened the door and let us through.

"I'll explain as soon as they're in bed," Abigail said shortly.

We put the little ones into the spare bed, then followed Aunt Claire into the kitchen. "Uncle Mark is away in New York this weekend," Aunt Claire said as we sat down.

"You want me to explain everything?" Abigail asked, ignoring her aunt's remark.

"Yes."

"Alright. Seven years ago, when I was six, my parents took me to the city. They took me out for dinner, and then told me that they were going to leave me at an orphanage. They couldn't care for me. I knew what it meant. I knew they didn't want me.

"I didn't say anything though. In fact, I didn't talk to anyone at all for three years after they left me. That's when the letters started to come.

"They said that they had made a horrible mistake, and would I please forgive them? They said they would come and get me in the blink of an eye, but they wanted to make sure that I would come with them. Didn't want to make the trip for nothing, I suppose.

"Well, I said no. I said that I'd got on fine without them for three years, and I could keep doing it. Miss Smith was nice to me, and I shared a room with some older girls who mothered me in a way my own mother never did.

"I've lived at the orphanage a few blocks away for seven years. Last year, Olivia and Natalie and I were put in the same room, and we all became good friends. Then, nine months ago, Katrina came.

"Miss Smith, the owner of the orphanage, left just three weeks ago. She is going to be married. But the woman who she hired in her place is mean and unfeeling. She put Rose, Penny, Ruby, and Sophia in our care as a punishment. Those are the girls sleeping upstairs.

"We've cared for them for two weeks, and the other day they got in a bit of mischief. Miss Malcolm was shouting at us, telling us we had no control over them, and I lost my temper. I left. That was today. Then, tonight, I came back to see if Natalie, Olivia, or Katrina wanted to come with me. I was going to run away. They all did, so we decided to take the little ones with us, instead of leaving them in the care of Miss Malcolm, who hates children.

"We needed a place to stay for

tonight, so I'm asking that you shelter us for the night, then we'll be off your hands."

Aunt Claire was crying silently. She stood up and crossed the room to Abigail. "Oh, Abbey. I'm so sorry," she said. "Why didn't you tell me?"

"Because there's nothing you can do. It was my parent's decision, and even if it was bad, that's what happened."

"You can stay here as long as you need. Those girls look about the same age as two of my little ones, so they'll fit right in. As for you older girls, I'm sure you won't be much trouble," said Aunt Claire.

"We'll do our best, but if we're any trouble to you, tell us," Olivia said.

"No trouble at all. I think you might have to sleep on the floor tonight, but tomorrow we'll get good, proper beds fixed up for you."

"No." Abigail was firm.

"But Abbey—" Aunt Claire started.

"No, I don't want to intrude on your family. You can't care for eight more children, and Uncle Mark wouldn't like it. I know you're trying to make up for what my mother and your sister did, but I don't need you to.

"Also, my name is Abigail not Abbey. Abbey was the name of the woman who abandoned me."

With that, she turned and stalked into the living room.

Chapter Sixteen

Aunt Claire took Olivia and Natalie into another spare bedroom to get a bed made up on the floor, but I hung back. I wanted to see if I could break through the armor that Abigail coated herself with.

I walked slowly into the living room and saw my friend curled in the corner of a sofa, shaking.

"Abigail?" I asked.

She looked up, and I saw that her face was streaked with tears.

"What's wrong?"

"Nothing. Nothing at all, I'm just fine." Abigail's voice was too high, like my own was after I learned that Father was dead.

I was down next to her.

"Why, Abigail? Why won't you let anyone in to help you? You keep everyone who loves you away."

"No one loves me."

"Yes they do. Your aunt loves you. Your friends love you. Rose and Penny and Ruby and Sophia love you. You just don't realize it because you push everyone away."

"You take that back, Katrina Evans! You have no idea! No idea!"

"Yes I do."

"Prove it."

So I told her. I told her how after Father died, I went to Helen's daughter's house, where I wasn't wanted. Then, I came to the orphanage. I had felt the same way as she did when Helen told me that I had to go to an orphanage. I had felt abandoned, and so completely alone.

And yes, my parents did not choose to leave me, but they were gone. There was no chance of a change of heart. Abigail's parents did love her, even if they had made a foolish decision.

"Being an orphan is horrible, but we have to stay together," I told her.

"Thank you for telling me that," Abigail whispered. "You're not like other people. Olivia and Natalie, although they're great, would never have come to me."

"You know, I had a friend, Mr. McCumber, back in Emerald Hills. Everyone thought he was looney, but I still became his friend."

"So you're saying I'm looney, Evans?" Abigail was smiling.

"No, I'm saying that I like to help people. Especially the ones who feel abandoned . . . Oh! I've just had a brilliant idea!"

"What?"

"We could go and live with Mr. McCumber! He has a huge house, and he wouldn't mind. We could take care of the little girls, and Emerald Hills is a lovely town!"

"I think I like this plan."

"Good. But let's talk it over in the morning. I'm exhausted."

"Sounds good."

We walked into the spare room, where Olivia and Natalie were lying in a nest of blankets and pillows on the floor. We crawled in with them and snuggled together, cozy and drowsy.

This was my new family. These girls were the sisters I never had.

Chapter Seventeen

"Yes, all we need are the train fares. We don't need you to come with us," I promised Aunt Claire. We had stayed an extra night, but now it was time to go. We were going to take the train to Emerald Hills, to go and live with Mr. McCumber. The reason why we had stayed an extra day was so that Aunt Claire could send a telegram to ask for

Mr. McCumber's consent. He had given it, so we were off to Emerald Hills.

We started down the street, waving behind us to Aunt Claire's children. Rose, Sophia, and the twins were neatly washed and dressed, and on this journey, they were walking, not sleeping.

We walked up to the train station and sat down on a bench. Abigail pulled out the coin purse that her aunt had given her and counted out enough for eight train tickets. "She gave us way too much!" Abigail said as she finished counting.

"We can get snacks!" Rose said.

Olivia sighed. "There's nothing we can do about it now except thank her in a letter. I'll go get the tickets. The train to Emerald Hills is supposed to come soon."

She took Sophia by the hand, and they walked to the ticket box.

I handed the twins a book that I had brought along, one with lots of pictures. Rose sat beside them, and we had peace for a little while.

Olivia and Sophia came back, and Olivia handed out the tickets.

A couple of other people wandered into the train station, and just as Rose, Sophia, and the twins had finished their book, the train pulled up.

We gathered up the little ones and herded them onto the train. We chose a compartment and sat down.

The train started to move and the twins started to wiggle. Sophia was too scared; she just looked around the train, utter fear in her eyes. Sophia hardly ever spoke, even though she was past three years old.

Rose sat tight in her seat, holding Sophia's hand. It was really funny how Rose acted as mother to the younger girl.

The twins had nobody to look after, and no thought of being frightened entered their heads. They wiggled and squirmed and giggled for a full ten minutes before the snack trolley appeared next to our compartment.

"Ooh! Can we get something?" Rose asked.

"They have candy!" called Penny.

"And cookies!" added Ruby.

Natalie looked at the rest of us, smiled, and stood up.

"Come with me," she said. "Do any of you guys want anything?" she asked Abigail, Olivia, and me.

"No, thanks."

"No."

"I'm good."

Natalie smiled and led the little girls over to the cart.

In a few moments they returned, each with an edible treasure. For sensible Rose, it was a small package with two cookies. For the twins, it was a bag of jellybeans each. And for Sophia, it was a chocolate chip cookie almost as large as her face.

Natalie had four chocolate bars in her hand, and she passed one to each of us. "In case you change your mind."

The train ride went smoothly for the most part, except once when we were stopping and Penny almost fell out the window. Ruby was so hysterical that it took a full ten minutes to calm her down and assure her that her twin was not going to die.

When we finally pulled into Emerald Hills, it was past lunchtime, and the treats of the morning were long forgotten. Everyone was hungry and grumpy, and Sophia was angry because she had been napping and the twins' rowdiness had woken her up.

But as the little town of Emerald Hills came into view, spirits lifted. I was happy beyond words. I was home.

We got off the train, and the four of us older girls each picked up a bag, grabbed the hand of a little girl, and together we left the station. Mr. McCumber was waiting right outside the station, looking very uncomfortable in his suit and top hat.

When I saw him, I let my bag drop and I ran to hug him. He was my first taste of the old comforts of home.

"I guess you're happy to see me?" he asked with a chuckle.

"Oh, yes!" I said. Then I remembered my manners. "Mr. McCumber, these are my friends, Olivia, Abigail, Natalie, Rose, Sophia, and the twins, Penny and Ruby."

"You've got quite the party! But I like it. I used to have a big fam—" he trailed off and turned toward his house. "Come this way!" he called.

"Don't mind him. He doesn't like to talk about his family. They all died, and left him alone," I explained.

"So he's an orphan?" Ruby asked

"No, grown-up people aren't orphans," said Abigail.

"Well I'm grown up—almost—and I'm an orphan!" said Penny.

I laughed, "You are not almost grown up, Penny. You have a long way to go."

We joined hands again and started after Mr. McCumber toward our new home.

Chapter Eighteen

Seven months and two weeks later.

I woke up to a wonderful sunrise. Beside me in bed, Abigail was still fast asleep. But I heard voices downstairs, so I pulled on my robe and slippers and slipped out of the room. I padded downstairs and into the kitchen to find six girls standing there, smiling. The tallest of the girls, blonde, serious Olivia, was holding a cake.

"Happy birthday!" all the girls said together.

Sophia flew at me and wrapped her pudgy arms around my legs. "Thank you!" I said, smiling at her and scooping her into my arms. I had forgotten, today was my fourteenth birthday.

"Where's Abigail?" Natalie asked.

"Still asleep. Why are you all up so early?" I asked. Usually I was the only older girl to get up at sunrise.

"Well, Abigail, Olivia, and I actually made the cake last night. The little ones woke us up this morning, instead of waking you. Obviously it didn't make much difference, since you're up at sunrise anyway," laughed Natalie.

I smiled.

"The 'little' ones woke me up too!" added Rose.

I nodded and ruffled her hair. Rose was only a year older than the twins, but at the grand old age of five, she considered herself much older than the rest of the "little ones."

"Where's Mr. McCumber?" I asked. Usually he was up before anyone.

"He's also still asleep. I thought maybe he was sick, because he never even sleeps until sunrise, but he said

he was okay, just a little tired," said Olivia.

"I want ca-ake!" sang Ruby. Penny joined in, and they chanted and danced around the kitchen table.

"Alright, alright. I'll cut the cake," I said. They stopped and climbed onto their little chairs at the table.

I cut seven slices and handed one to each of my friends, then I took one for myself and sat down at the table.

We ate our cake, and just as I was polishing off the last crumb, Abigail came in. She wished me a happy birthday, and took a slice of cake and began to eat. I smiled. Abigail was definitely not a morning person.

After breakfast, I helped Ruby get dressed and braid her hair. Ruby, Penny, and Rose all attended school, but Sophia, who was too young, stayed home.

I dressed and readied myself too, and the seven of us started out. Sophia stayed with Mr. McCumber because he could manage one three-year-old, even at his old age. At school, we met up with my old friend, Sara. When we had returned to Emerald Hills, Sara and I had not been as close. I had been gone for nine months, and a lot had changed for me. Plus, I had Abigail, Olivia, and Natalie. But soon, Sara plucked up the courage to come talk to us, and now during school hours, the five of us were inseparable.

The younger girls had made some friends too, especially one girl named Eloise. Eloise was five, but unlike Rose, did not think herself too high and mighty to play with "little baby four-year-olds."

School was different than it had been in the orphanage, but there was a different teacher than the one I had known before in Emerald Hills, and her teaching methods were much like Peggy Rogerson's.

After school, we went back home. Mr. McCumber had taken Sophia for a walk, so Olivia got Rose and the twins set up to learn the lessons that their teacher had assigned them to do at home while Natalie, Abigail, and I began to make dinner.

There was a cut of pork for dinner, along with lots of vegetables, and the leftover cake for dessert. Mr. McCumber came back around five o'clock, and the younger girls went out to play in the yard.

We ate dinner at the big table in the dining room, and afterward, we sat in the living room.

"We have another surprise for you, Katrina," Sophia told me solemnly.

"Sophia!" said Natalie. "You weren't supposed to tell"

Then, to my surprise and delight, each person handed me a small package. I opened them one at a time, oohing and ahhing over the pictures drawn painstakingly with Sophia's pencils. Mr. McCumber had gotten me a book, another one by L.M. Montgomery. This one was called *Emily of New Moon*.

Olivia had gotten me a new set of pencils, Natalie had gotten me a journal, and Abigail had gotten me yet another L.M. Montgomery book; this one was called *The Story Girl*. "Thank you so much, everyone!" I said, hugging each one in turn. "This has been the best birthday ever."

"I'm glad, but we'd better get the little ones to bed. I think that Sophia is going to fall asleep in my lap," laughed Olivia.

I picked up Ruby and kissed her chubby cheek. Then, I gathered my gifts under my other arm and followed Abigail up to the twins' room.

Unlike at Miss Malcolm's where we had all shared a room meant for four girls instead of eight, there were four rooms for us. The twins had a room together, with two small beds covered in pink quilts.

I helped Ruby get into her night clothes and brush her hair while Abigail did the same to Penny. I tucked Ruby into bed, then went back downstairs.

"Do you guys want to go for a walk?" Natalie asked as she came down from putting Rose to bed.

We all agreed, so we started off.

I was strongly reminded, as we walked down the street, of the time that I had first met Olivia Winslow, Abigail Hayes, and Natalie Gardiner.

It was in school at the orphanage, and I had walked in, scared and timid. Natalie had immediately welcomed me into their ranks. Olivia and Abigail were a bit more unsure, but soon, we were the best of friends. And now, we were living like sisters.

"I wonder what would have happened if Miss Malcolm had never taken in Rose, Sophia, and the twins and put us in charge of raising them," said Olivia, looking up at the sky.

"We would still be in the city in the orphanage, that's what!" said Natalie.

"If I hadn't run out on Miss Malcolm, we would still be there," Abigail added.

"At the time, I was furious with you for not keeping your own anger in check. Now I'm so glad that your temper broke out and that you ran away." I laughed.

We walked in silence for a while, and soon found ourselves on top of Elk Mountain. Elk Mountain was not a real mountain, just a rather large hill.

"Let's just lie here and look at the stars for a while," suggested Abigail.

Without a word, I sat down, then laid back and stretched out on the grass. Above me, the stars twinkled like thousands and thousands of candles, cutting through the inky blackness. Olivia pointed out Ursa Major and Orion's Belt and the Big Dipper. Then we just lay there in silence.

The sky seemed to change from navy blue, with the tiniest bit of light from the sun, to a blackness that seemed to have no end. It just went on forever and ever.

"Natalie's asleep," Abigail whispered after a while.

"We should head back. Mr. McCumber will get worried," I said.

Olivia sat up and gently shook Natalie's shoulder.

"Hey, Nat," she whispered. "We have to go back home."

Natalie moaned and sat up.

Abigail and I sat up too, and we all slowly rose to our feet. It was the kind of night where you felt like a sloth, slow and with no rush. We walked slowly back home, through the streets that were just as black as the sky because the lights in the windows had gone out.

But when we turned onto our street, I could see that our kitchen light cut through the blackness,

shining like a lighthouse beam, guiding us.

We went in through the kitchen door. Mr. McCumber was sitting at the table, drinking tea. "I thought I'd wait up for you. Didn't know you were going to be this long," he said with a chuckle.

"Sorry," I said.

"I'm going to go to bed," Natalie said through a yawn.

"I'll join you," Olivia decided.

"Me too," agreed Abigail. "What about you, Katrina?"

"I'm going to stay down here for a little while," I said. There was something Mr. McCumber wanted to say. I could always tell, and I guessed that since he hadn't said it yet, he wanted to say it to just me.

Olivia, Abigail, and Natalie headed upstairs, but I sat down on one of the kitchen stools. "What's wrong?" I asked.

He looked up at me, and I was surprised to see tears sparkling in his eyes. He whispered something, but I couldn't hear it.

"Could you say that again?" I asked.

He took a deep breath.

"They have found my daughter."

Chapter Nineteen

"Wait . . . what?" I asked, unsure whether I had heard him right.

"A Miss Annelise McCumber was recently found . . . Actually, I'd better tell you the whole story, from the beginning."

He poured me a cup of tea, refilled his own, and began.

"It turns out that Annelise was not killed in the train incident as I had been told. She was taken into intensive care at the hospital. They did think she would die. But she didn't. She was in a coma, and when she woke up, she had no memory. No memory at all. She didn't know who she was, or how she had been injured. She was like a baby; she didn't know how to feed herself or dress herself.

"She was taken in by an elderly couple who live in New York. They treated her like their own daughter. She has lived for the past fourteen years under the name Emmalyn Gregory. Recently, a good friend of mine was visiting New York and happened to run into Annelise in a bookshop. He recognized her instantly, but thought he was seeing a ghost.

"He introduced himself and asked her name. She said that she was told her name was Emmalyn Gregory. He asked what she meant what she meant 'that she was told' that was her name, and she explained what had happened. My friend then understood what had actually happened. He told her that her given name was actually Annelise McCumber, and that he was good friends with her father—me.

"Annelise is coming on the next train to Emerald Hills. She will arrive tomorrow morning."

"Oh, Mr. McCumber!" I didn't know what to say. I remembered when I had first met Mr. McCumber, how he had confused me with his daughter Annelise, who had supposedly died when she was my age.

Now, though, that wouldn't happen. Annelise would be twenty-seven, no longer a little girl.

"Is she coming to live here?" I asked.

"If you and your friends will have her."

"Oh! Yes! Anyway, she's your daughter, and this is your house. You don't have to ask us. But do you mind if I tell Abigail and Olivia and Natalie what you told me?"

"Of course that's alright."

"Then I'd better be going to bed. I'm tired."

I hugged Mr. McCumber, then turned and started up the stairs.

When I got into my room, Abigail was still awake, sitting on her bed.

"Why did you stay down there?" she asked.

"Mr. McCumber had something to tell me. Abigail, guess what?"

I told her all about how Mr. McCumber used to confuse me with Annelise, and how Annelise was now found, and was coming tomorrow.

"Oh! It's just like a storybook!" Abigail said when I had finished. "But we'd really better get to bed, if she's coming on the early train."

I nodded, and pulled on my pajamas. I slipped into bed, shivering happily with excitement.

The next morning, at exactly three past eight, Mr. McCumber, Olivia, Natalie, Abigail, Rose, Penny, Ruby, Sophia, and I were waiting on a bench. The train had just pulled up, and passengers were spilling out of the doors. Mr. McCumber was glancing around anxiously.

Just then, a thin young woman wove through the crowd and stopped

Annelise took over the kitchen and would not allow anyone in.
She stayed in there for four hours, and when we were finally allowed
back in the kitchen, it looked like a scene from a painting.

in front of us.

"Annelise?" Mr. McCumber asked hoarsely.

"Father?"

Mr. McCumber stood up and embraced his daughter, but quickly pulled back.

"Do you remember me?" he asked.

"Yes ... When your friend, Mr. Stewart, told me that my name was Annelise McCumber, everything came rushing back. You, and Mother and all my brothers ... But what happened to the rest of them? Why are you the only one here?"

Mr. McCumber did not answer.

"Annelise, your mother died in the train accident. And your brothers died in the war," I said quietly, when it was clear that Mr. McCumber was not going to answer.

"Oh," she said quietly.

"We must put our sadness behind us though," said Mr. McCumber suddenly. "This is my new family. It seems that it was my destiny to be surrounded by womenfolk. I was the only boy in my family, I had six older sisters, and now I'll have nine girls living with me!" He laughed.

We walked home, everyone laughing and talking. Annelise said that she had experience helping with young children, and that she could take some of the work of raising the little ones off our hands.

"You've become mothers before your time," she said.

"I am not little!" protested Rose.

When we got home, Annelise took over the kitchen and would not allow anyone in. She stayed in there for four hours, and when we were finally allowed back in the kitchen, it looked like a scene from a painting.

There were all sorts of foods. There were pies and tarts and jars of jams and jellies, there was a whole roast turkey (I have no idea where she got that from), and there was a cake that would rival the four-tiered ones Mrs. Howard used to make when she was trying to outshine Helen with bakery accomplishments.

Dinner was a perfect feast, and after dinner, Annelise called all of us girls in to help with the cleaning up.

"That's not fair! We didn't do any of the cooking!" protested Natalie, but Annelise just laughed and said that we'd better help, because otherwise we would have to do all the cooking and all the cleanup next time.

While we were cleaning, we talked, telling each other about ourselves. Just as we untied our aprons and hung them up, Annelise said, "I think that you girls will be like the sisters I always wished I had. Even though I'm older than you in body, I'm still your age at heart. Will you let me into your games and secrets? I would so love to be like a big sister to you all."

"I'd like that," Abigail said quietly. At one time, I would have thought Abigail would be the last to agree to Annelise's statement, and when she did, she would do it grudgingly. But Abigail had changed more than any of us since we had left the orphanage.

She no longer coated herself in invincible armor; she let us in, let us be there for her just like she was always there for us.

"I'd like that too," Olivia said.

"Me too!" Natalie added.

"That would be really nice," I said.

Rose, who was the youngest girl in the kitchen just then, gave her answer with no words, just a big hug around Annelise's waist.

Annelise was going to sleep on the floor in my and Abigail's room until we could get the last bedroom fixed up for her.

As we undressed and put on our nightclothes, we talked of all the things we meant to do. Annelise would not come to school, of course. But after school and on weekends we had plenty of time for adventures.

Annelise wanted to act as our big sister, and she did a good job. She didn't say any of our ideas were silly, although plenty of them were. And she was just as lively as any of us. What she had said was true: she was older than us in age, but the same age as us at heart. And that night, I fell asleep happier than I had been since Father died.

Because I knew for certain now that I had found my family.

Epilogue

Six years later…

The house was still the same. It was still filled with memories, and with laughter. But the man of the house was gone. Mr. McCumber had gone out of life like he had lived in it: quiet, and by himself. He died in his sleep.

I was sad of course. But it wasn't the kind of sadness I had drowned in when Father died. This sadness was more bearable.

And I had people to share the sadness with. I was going to stay with my new family as long as could be permitted.

Annelise was married; she was no longer Annelise McCumber, but Annelise Drake. She no longer lived with us in the big house where her father had lived, but with her husband and her daughter in a small cottage right next door.

My friends and I were getting ready to go off to college. Abigail and I were twenty and going into our junior year.

Olivia was nineteen, and about to begin her sophomore year.

And Natalie, the youngest of us four, was about to start her very first year of college.

Annelise had promised that while we older girls were at college, the little girls could live with her, Mr. Drake, and Baby Francis. But the "little girls" were not so little anymore. Sophia, who had really been a baby when we moved in with Mr. McCumber, was nine years old.

The day after Mr. McCumber died, I discovered the rocking chair where he used to sit and play his guitar, and I discovered his old guitar, hidden away in a closet. He had hardly played for my friends and me while we lived here. I chuckled to think how much work we must have been to him, four half-grown girls trying to raise four babies all by themselves. But, that day, I decided to teach myself how to play. I would play all of Mr. McCumber's old songs, if only I could learn.

It turned out that I didn't have

to teach myself, though. Mr. Drake, Annelise's husband, was a musician, and he taught me to play exactly like Mr. McCumber once did. Now, I could play all of his songs, just as I had hoped. And even Rose, who considered herself far too grown up to play very much (even though she was only eleven) liked to listen to the guitar, and to Olivia's clear, sweet voice singing along.

Often, I would play the first song that I ever remembered Mr. McCumber singing, and when I did, I reminded myself of him sometimes, although I was not lonely as he had been. But there I was, sitting in the rocking chair where he'd once sat and playing one of his favorite songs, "Church Street Blues":

> *Lord I been hangin' out of town in*
> *that low-down rain*
> *Watchin' good-time Charlie, friend,*
> *is drivin' me insane*
> *Down on shady Charlotte Street*
> *the green lights look red*
> *Wish I was back home on the farm,*
> *in my feather bed*
>
> *Get myself a rockin' chair*
> *To see if I can lose*
> *Them thin dime-hard times*
> *'Ell on Church Street blues*

Night (Acrylic)
Rosemary Brandon, 10
Nashville, TN

An excerpt from
The Other Realm

Winner of our 2020 book contest

By Tristan Hui, 14
Menlo Park, CA

The Other Realm will be released on September 1, 2021.

You can preorder the book at our store: **stonesoupstore.com**

Chapter One

The mind of Azalea Morroe's father was coming apart. Gradually, and only at the seams, but coming apart all the same—and that was where the adventure began.

Henry Morroe was not terribly old, nor terribly unhealthy. A researcher in an astronomical laboratory, he was both fervently passionate about his work and blissfully oblivious to his unpopularity at the place. Henry had always been of an eccentric manner, and because of this, no one really noticed that anything was wrong. For what was now out of order in his mind was assumed to have always been that way. Eccentricity was not a welcome or valued trait in Montero; the little family spent most of their time shut up in the little flat they shared, except for when Azalea went to school over the hill and her father to work—when he went to work. Lately, it had not been so.

Lately, Henry Morroe was in his study from sunrise till sunset, combing over maps and taking notes from books, sticking tabs of paper to the walls, and perpetually adding to the jumbo fold-out poster board that was to save him from being laid off. In truth, it was more of a firing than a layoff, because the research company had never been a fan of Henry Morroe—although he did good work, they were much more preoccupied with their image than the accuracy of their research. They had finally found someone better—rather, someone much wealthier and more popular—to analyze and compare the data collected by the many enormous telescopes in the lab. Sure, the results might be sorely lacking in accuracy, but the image the lab projected onto the astronomical research industry would be brightened tenfold. It was a worthy switch.

However, Henry Morroe had heard of this plan some weeks back—listening with an antique ear trumpet pressed to the keyhole of his supervisor's office—and the news had derailed any other train of thought completely. They had granted him a temporary leave while they set

Although Azalea Morroe was no longer a child, she had not yet discerned the difference between insanity and sanity, had not yet realized that her father was edging closer and closer to the former.

the other guy up in Henry's office, and Azalea's father had taken that time to formulate a plan guaranteed to get his job back.

This plan revolved around the information concealed in a dusty old volume, one that Azalea was reading while she stood in front of the bathroom mirror brushing her teeth. *All About the Two Realms*, by Dr. Arnold Colton, was a book with a history deeper than most. Eccentricity did not prompt celebration in Montero, and Dr. Arnold Colton had written a very eccentric book.

All About the Two Realms introduced the concept that there was more than one realm in existence, that there was another realm below the one in which Montero sprawled, made up of people similar to humans but not entirely the same. This was possibly the detail that sank the idea—no one in Montero was ready to welcome an alien race to their city. According to Dr. Colton, if you believed in both realms, it was possible to travel between them when a black moon coincided with a low tide—and in the lower realm, it was common knowledge that the upper one existed.

Dr. Arnold Colton and his book were banned from Montero and the surrounding region almost immediately after its release, the publishers pulled out of their contract with the city's library, and most anyone who had previously been fascinated by this new worldview stowed the book hastily somewhere dark and never spoke of their infatuation with it again—but Henry Morroe felt no shame in taking instruction from a banned book, and neither did his daughter.

It was said that this realm held an island that provided the perfect star-charting vantage point, with spectacular views of a few planets not yet known to the people of Montero. The sleek black rock rose up out of the water and gave way quickly to dense forest—not a grain of sand to be found, despite the vast desert that stretched out across the strait. Apparently, this enclave was no tropical vacation spot but the trade capital of the realm and abuzz with all nature of activities. People of all shapes and sizes flocked to the isle to sell a variety of colorful, extraordinary goods, and many of them liked it so much that they simply stayed. The capital city loomed not far from the harbor, and beyond that green hills, interrupted only by the occasional tiny hamlet, ambled along, grasses swaying. Not many people lived around there, and the sky was pitch black—that, Dr. Colton claimed, was the place where you could see the stars with your naked eye.

Henry was certain that if he were to bring information from this wonderland to his lab, they would surely take him back. And Azalea, wishing to bring her father happiness in any way possible, agreed.

Although Azalea Morroe was no longer a child, she had not yet discerned the difference between insanity and sanity, had not yet realized that her father was edging closer and closer to the former. She still took his word for truth without a second thought, looking to him for guidance as a flower to the sun—unaware that he too relied on her.

Most of the time, the two lived contentedly together in their little flat, and for the fifteen years that Azalea had been alive, the occupancy of the place had never exceeded two people. Her mother had run off as soon as Azalea was born, but she was missed as often as father and daughter fought. There were no photographs of her, and Azalea often wondered if her mother had given her the hair like coffee grounds that kinked tightly when it was braided, or the shortness of her figure—Henry was straight-haired, previously blond, and tall. But for the size of their home, the number of inhabitants was plenty. There was one bathroom at the end of the hall, then the study, then Henry's room, then Azalea's across from it, and finally the tiny kitchen and the living room. Books and papers covered every available surface. If you looked out the living room window, you could see one of Montero's cobblestone streets below, and the window box of the family who lived in the flat beneath them filled to the brim with hardy flowers. The Morroes had filled their window box with books.

Across the street was another row of rather paltry apartments, and over their horizontal gray rooftops the desert unfurled, shining like gold in the sunrise. Recently, the perpetual haze blanketing the landscape had thickened into swirling sand, a subtle indicator of the tumult to come.

Though it had not yet happened in Azalea's lifetime, everyone in Montero knew that a long, harsh drought like this one meant a sandstorm was coming. It always began slowly like this—the haze thickening, grasses dying, sand sweeping up into the elevated town as the tempest gained intensity to the breaking point. Then, what felt like half of the desert would rush over them, shattering any windows that had not been boarded up, tearing off any pieces of flimsy apartment roof that had not been battened down, and wrecking anyone who had failed to stay inside. But for now, Montero's residents had only an abundance of sand as evidence of this phenomenon, and the grains could be found lining windowsills, creeping under doors, in everyone's hair, and settling in little drifts anywhere the broom couldn't reach, which was most everywhere—at least in the Morroe household.

Over the years, the apartment had fallen into a state of mild disrepair. One set of the living room lights had stopped working nearly ten years ago, but no one had bothered to replace them because the room was so small that it hardly mattered. The study windows refused to open, but that also didn't matter because large bookshelves smothered them. When it rained—however scarcely that happened in such a place—the doors swelled in their frames and had to be shoved in order to get into the next room, and the front door only occasionally locked (no one ever came calling at the Morroes', so that didn't matter either). Sometimes the floorboards in the hallway went shaky and creaked when you stepped on them, but neither Henry nor Azalea noticed when crossing the floor in dim light anymore. Azalea only noticed this time because— and thankfully she didn't still have her toothbrush in her mouth—the wood sank away, and she fell straight through the floor into the dark.

Chapter Two

The inky blackness swirling around Azalea lifted almost as quickly as it had fallen. The world spun as her feet slammed into hard, dry earth, the impact forcing her to her knees. The first thing Azalea noticed was that *All About the Two Realms* was gone; she must have dropped it while falling through the floor. But she had not fallen to the floor below her Montero apartment. No—when she looked up, this was not Montero at all. Azalea was crouched on the hard, dry ground of an expansive desert, the air hazy and landscape painted in muted hues. She was not alone here—a line of rather bedraggled people was making its way into a rectangular building through wide double doors, a sign over which read "Cambelt Refugee Shelter," and to the left of it, a yellowing field was packed with multicolored tents, more disheveled families bustling into, out of, and around them. Azalea knew the word "Cambelt" from somewhere, surely—but who knew where. The sight of the crowd extinguished

any belief she might've had that she was anywhere familiar, for Montero didn't have any sort of refugee shelter, and no one ever crossed *their* desert on foot.

"Come in, come in, refugees! It's alright. You'll be safe here." A plump, rosy-cheeked woman was beckoning Azalea and a few others who had not yet joined the line toward her, a small smile on her face. Her brown cotton dress with peach-colored polka dots was wrinkled and the white apron she tied over it stained with dirt, but she looked to be in charge, so Azalea straightened and made her way through the queueing people to her.

"Excuse me, but where is this? Where am I? I'm from Montero, and I need to get home."

The woman laid a warm hand onto Azalea's upper arm. She continued to smile and spoke not unkindly, but up close her expression seemed strangely emotionless; her eyes seemed to have next to nothing behind them. "Here, hon. Come in. I'll get you a blanket, some water . . ."

Azalea pulled her arm away, and her heart began to pound. She schooled herself—*calm down, you aren't in danger yet, don't be silly, this woman thinks you're someone else, that's all*—but it wasn't much use, and the helper's taciturn manner did her no favors. "No, I want to know where I am. I'm not from Cambelt. I don't even know where that is– "

"You're in Ambergard, honey. You'll be safe here, warm and dry."

"I-I'm sorry, I think this is a mistake—I'm completely fine. I don't need blankets or water or anything. I'm not from Cambelt. I'm from

Was she in another realm? *The* other realm?

Montero, and I want to go home."
Azalea was fighting to keep the
childish edge out of her voice, trying
to suppress the panic bubbling in her
stomach. But even as she protested,
the woman took hold of her arm again
and led her into the building.

It was like an enormous school
gymnasium, with cots folded out
in long rows to the right and an
impromptu food bar set up on the
left. Plastic chairs lined each wall.
Exhausted and dirty people crowded
the place, families sitting together on
the beds or single men and women
slumped on the sidelines. No one
seemed injured, only gravely fatigued
and overcrowded. People were
crying and some were sitting on the
floor between the beds and in the
walkways, for in most places there
was no room left for dignity.

What was happening in Cambelt?
A war? A natural disaster? Where
was Cambelt, and what was it
anyway?

But Azalea realized she could
now answer the last question for
herself. Cambelt was the astronomical
wonderland mentioned in Arnold
Colton's book, and it was the very
place her father wished to travel to
and gather information from. Cambelt
was supposedly somewhere in the
realm that sat below the human one.

Was she in another realm? *The*
other realm?

"Sit down here, honey." The rosy-
cheeked woman derailed her train of
thought, gesturing to a plastic chair.

Dazed, Azalea sat watching silently
as the helper was swallowed up by the
crowd. If she had somehow landed
herself in the other realm, then these
people were not human. They looked
human. Would *they* believe in another
realm? Could they, or would they,
help her return home? She almost
laughed. Just a few hours ago she had
been wishing to get out of the world
she was currently in, to a place where
there was a job for her father and no
dust storm on the horizon. Now that
she might actually be there, the only
thing she wanted was to return to her
cramped apartment.

"Here you go, hon." The rosy-
cheeked woman was back, carrying a
heavy woolen blanket and a chipped
coffee mug full of water, her voice
jerking Azalea from her speculations
again.

Azalea accepted the mug but
shook her head at the blanket,
interjecting, "I'm not from Cambelt.
I've already told you. I'm from
Montero, and I haven't suffered
through anything. I just want to go
home to my father."

"Honey, you're safe here. I'm sure
you're exhausted after such a long
journey, but there aren't any beds
open now. If I see one, I'll let you
know." The woman still seemed oddly
disconnected and cool, as though she
wasn't really absorbing what Azalea
was telling her, or like she didn't
actually care.

"No, I haven't taken any sort of
journey! I'm completely fine! I'm from
Montero, not Cambelt."

"Just rest now, alright? The island
has many other cities. You need not live
in the capital to receive shelter here."

Azalea could feel her heart thundering in her chest again, panic rising like bile in her throat. "I don't live on an island! I swear I don't even know where Cambelt is—"

But the woman had shoved the blanket in her lap, patted her on the shoulder, and disappeared again into the throng.

Chapter Three

Sunny had left hastily for work that morning, eager to be out of the claustrophobic house and blanketing noise. She hadn't cared that she would end up in a place noisier and more crowded, nor that her breath sparkled in the dawn chill. No, she had only cared for the walk. Rucksack tightly secured and thumbs hooked in her pockets, she could gaze out over the ridge and into the desert below. These fifteen early morning minutes were of complete, solitary peace—something rare as rain in this time and place.

It had not rained in Ambergard for 471 days, the longest stretch recorded for more than a century. There was nothing to temper the dust or the heat, and yet the other extreme was being reached just across the strait. In Cambelt, annual floods were worse than they had been in over a century, affecting not only the rural communities but some of the hamlets too, and the refugees that trekked across the desert to seek shelter in Ambergard—usually filling the recreational field with a tent city— had overflowed into the community building and were sucking away what little resources her desert town possessed.

But Sunny could push thoughts of this out of her head during the walk. She did not have to dwell on how pale little Theodore had become, how skinny Addi was, or how tired Eli always appeared to be. Her mother was trying her hardest, but it wasn't enough for them. Theo was only six months old, and the attention Mama bestowed upon him in a desperate attempt to salvage his health was attention stolen from four-year-old Addi, nine-year-old Eli, and fifteen-year-old Sunny herself. And now her mother wanted Sunny to leave them all.

Though Mama wanted Sunny to leave "only for the health of the rest of the family," even in the words with which she justified her wish she planted seeds of doubt in her daughter's mind. Was there really another reason she wanted Sunny gone? In times of such scarce resources, was her eldest daughter the one she would let go of? Even the reason behind her impending journey was centered upon someone else: she was to travel to Cambelt and hunt down her older brother, Jamone, to convince him to return home and repair the water systems of Ambergard.

Jamone was Mama's first child, a dark-haired boy of curiosity and goodwill. She'd done as much as she could for him, but Jamone had grown impatient with the lack of opportunity that Ambergard presented to him. A tiny desert-bordered town known only as a travelers' stop gave him no way to follow his long-nurtured dream of becoming a marine geologist. When he was fifteen, he ran away to Cambelt, where he wished to study. No one in Ambergard had any idea whether he had done it, or heard from him since.

This was the only side that Sunny had seen of him, a bitter one her mother had shared only as a cautionary tale of ungratefulness. At least, it was the only one she trusted. Sunny seemed to remember times with Jamone on the ridge where she now walked, crouching just off the road. He would trace patterns in the dust, kindly explaining about erosion and water currents. But her mother's negative and bold recollections had long since stamped her own pleasant and misty ones to ash, and the only thing she felt now when confronted with seeing him again was a kind of dull resentment. He was an undeserving, deceitful boy hiding behind pleasantries and charlatanry from his family and his home—at least, that was what her mother wished her to think.

As much as she hated the idea, worried sick of something happening in her absence, Sunny knew that Mama had already won the battle. She had never been one to lose a fight, the only one she had ever lost being Jamone's running away—yet another reason for Sunny to despise her brother. But as far as Sunny could tell, as much as Mama urged her to leave, she didn't actually have any idea how she would get her daughter across the desert. Either that, or her mother didn't want her to go.

They were washing the dishes after dinner when Sunny had broached the subject again, a few days after Mama had pitched the plan that had left her daughter's stomach sour and roiling.

"Mama, um, about the plan to find Jamone—uh, well, how am I gonna get to Cambelt? I mean, I can't really walk all the way there, and even if I could, I can't swim, and I don't know how to use a boat. I'd be stuck on the coast."

Her mother had given a small sigh and turned her face away, twisting the cold-water handle around as far as it would go—hot had stopped working years ago. What had been a feeble but relatively steady stream of dirty water from the tap became a sputtering explosion of brown, spattering them both with muddiness. Sunny had reached across the metal basin to turn down the flow, but with a rattling noise somewhere in the innards of the piping, followed by the gush of roaring water, a clot of sand shot from the faucet and slid down the drain, dissolving as soon as the murky flow from the now-cleared faucet hit it. The harsh noise of the water flooding the sink had made Mama shudder, and Sunny had seen for the umpteenth time that day how tired she looked, face graying, like her hair, with exhaustion and pools of shadow beneath her eyes that gave her whole face a deflated look. Suddenly she had been struck with a pang of guilt, knowing she had done something to make her mother's life harder, to make her even more fatigued than she had been since her husband left last year.

She shook her head. "Never mind, Mama. We'll talk about it later. I can finish this. You go take a rest, 'kay?"

Her mother had nodded gratefully

at this and murmured her thanks, wiping her hands dry on her dress and leaving Sunny standing there with a sponge and a greasy plate, staring blankly out the grimy window at the sunset with no less of a sick stomach than before.

Thinking that this was just a one-time situation, she had tried to discuss the trip again when her mother seemed in better spirits, but to no avail. Each time Sunny had been stopped by a "Honey, I've got to go nurse Theo now. We can talk some other time," or Addi needed to be dressed for bed, or the tap needed to be turned on high enough to mask noise, or dinner needed to be cooked, or she needed to focus on the entirely silent and mindless task of ironing lest one of Eli's shirts get a hole burnt through. In any case, Sunny was realizing that Mama didn't *want* to know when she was leaving, for one reason or the other, and so she stopped trying and started hoping that the day for her trip would just never come around.

The sun had risen entirely above the horizon now, flooding the sand with golden light. The low-built community center came into view down the slight incline, and as Sunny watched, the lights came on, their glare muted by the thick panes of the high windows.

The sparse grass that used to line the edge of the road here had died away with the rain, replaced with yet more of the sand that was gritted into every nook and cranny these days. The avenue ran from dirt to worn asphalt, growing hot beneath the soles of Sunny's sandals as they slapped the pavement leading to the low building's side door.

She slid in behind the food bar, quick to exchange her bag for a pile of blankets and head toward the public entranceway.

"Sunny!" Miss Genevieve was hurrying toward her, arms outstretched and looking hassled. "Here, give me one of those—there's a girl I just brought in delirious with dehydration and exhaustion—and go watch the door, will you? New arrivals are coming this way. I could see them on the horizon."

"I'm on it, Miss Genevieve."

She was used to the hectic, no-pleasantries-involved nature of the volunteer center by now, and the often strained, no-nonsense demands of her boss. It was only on weekends that she caught glimpses of the other side of Miss Genevieve as she bustled into her office for more supplies, letting down her guard a little, smiling and humming along with the radio. The weekday shift of volunteers organized files in her office on weekends and got paid for it, many of them—Sunny included—fulfilling their role as sole breadwinner for their families. But they could only be paid on Saturdays and Sundays if they agreed to volunteer with the refugees for the rest of the week, something Sunny was glad to do anyway since it gave her an excuse to get away. The weekend shifts had many more hands because numbers were bolstered by the kids lucky enough to still be going to school, and there were a lot more of them than the breadwinners. Miss Genevieve could relax on the weekends, and so could the school kids—their load wasn't stretched so thin. Sunny found envy in the pit of her stomach at this, but then she thought of Mama's face every time she brought home her paycheck and smiled a little instead.

Anyway, sitting on the desk in a relatively cool, dim room and filing papers with some people she had a bit of common ground with, humming along with the tunes on the radio and remembering the clinks of the coins that she was earning, beat sitting in a dark house, hot and cramped, and singing Addi to sleep, getting nothing in return but more time to gaze at her mother's sorry face.

The glare of the sun shimmered into mirages against the sand, but Sunny had no time to watch them rise. The group her boss had mentioned was drawing closer, a small one lurching along in laborious, stilted steps. Sunny had arrived just in time to see them stumble and barely avoid collapse, pushing forward through the murk of exhaustion.

She hurried forward, tightening her grip on the blankets and squinting her eyes against the sun's brilliant light. Ahead of the party walked another figure, dressed in the brown traveling cloak so many of the refugees arrived in. She strode purposefully toward the building, and Sunny slowed to watch her—so unusual was her gait compared to the other refugees'. She couldn't have been more than twenty-five, and it was only when she drew closer that this woman's fatigue became apparent. Her face was smudged with dust, and though she was quite tall and looked commanding from a distance, Sunny could see now how she trembled slightly and pulled the government-issued garment tight around her thin shoulders. Her hair was long and wavy, but the chocolate strands were matted and looked damp and dull.

"Excuse me. Do you need help?"

It was only now that she seemed to notice Sunny and turned to look her up and down—that was when Sunny first saw her eyes. They were hazel, and much brighter than normal. They also seemed to be burning holes straight into Sunny's soul, and she took a step back, hugging the blankets to her chest like a shield, suddenly all too conscious of the old, worn overalls and stained plaid flannel she had pulled on this morning without a second thought. But this last self-judgement was quickly rationalized—it wasn't like she had anything else. Sunny looked away, and the woman spoke.

"No, I'm alright. I go through those doors?"

"Yeah, um, in there someone can get you water, a blanket, and some soup."

"Thank you."

She was not unkind, but all the same it was a relief when she turned away to continue into the building. Sunny continued to the weakened group of refugees with her blankets, blinking away the image of the woman's hazel eyes.

Back inside, having safely delivered two exhausted men to the soup kitchen, Sunny caught a glimpse of the woman again, cloak hood down

The fire in her eyes had been doused, and now she just looked lost, desperate.

and her unkempt hair completely exposed. She was arguing with a distressed-looking girl in a white sweater with a wide green stripe across the front.

The woman was not holding a blanket, a mug of water, or a bowl of today's soup. Sometimes they arrived like this: emaciated and sapped of energy, yet for no apparent reason refusing help. In these cases, it was a volunteer's job to talk them into submission—and today it would be no easy task. Sunny sighed and began to push her way through the crowd, shimmying between rows of beds and stepping over legs and arms until she reached the girl in the green-and-white striped sweater—and her apparent opponent.

The girl was evidently attempting to give the woman with the hazel eyes her bed. The woman—against all reason—would not take it. Sunny stood between the refugees for a moment, watching the argument like a sports game and attempting to interject.

"Um, miss—"

"I swear, you must keep your bed. You are young and precious—"

"I'm young and resilient. Plus, I don't even need this stupid bed! I'm not hurt!"

The girl's eyes were blazing, but the woman Sunny had met outside refused to drop her gaze, and eventually the younger one faltered— in her stare, not her argument.

"Excuse me—" Sunny began.

"You must keep it for exhaustion.

I will take a chair. Your family is not with you? Stay in one place so they can find you again!"

"Ma'am—"

"I haven't got any family with me. Now please take the bed! I haven't got any use for it, but you certainly do!"

"Rubbish." The suggestion of weakness seemed to have sparked something in her, and what had been an argument rooted in generosity was now quickly evolving into one of strength. This woman was ready to end it, and Sunny opened her mouth to try again, but to no avail.

"I will leave this bed to you and find a chair. I am fine."

She swept her brown cloak about her again and stalked off.

The girl in the green-and-white striped sweater groaned, covering her face with her hands and flopping back onto the white sheets. That was the way Sunny felt, but she was working, and it wasn't even lunch break. The girl looked to be about the same age as Sunny herself, with frizzy, dark-brown hair kinked into braids and a smattering of freckles bridging her nose.

"Er … can I help you?"

"I don't even know." The girl pulled herself up into a sitting position rather more laboriously than seemed necessary, but if there was one thing Sunny had learned on this job, it was not to judge. "Would you just listen for a minute?"

"Um … alright."

"Okay." The fire in her eyes had been doused, and now she just looked lost, desperate. "Well. So. So, I'm sure you've heard this before, but I swear I'm not from Cambelt. Not anywhere near there either, because I have no idea where it is or how to get to it. And also, I have no idea how I got here, none at all. I mean, I know it doesn't really make sense, but I was walking down the hallway in my apartment and I sort of fell through the floor? I swear it's true! I'm not delirious or anything!"

The color had risen into her cheeks now, and she wrung her hands in her lap. "My father's back there, where I live, and I need to get back to him. I've got to. I don't know what's happening that's sending all these refugees here, but it hasn't happened to me. I'm totally fine, really, but I think I maybe come from another—another realm?"

Sunny stared at the girl, struggling to absorb the fast-moving information, until she remembered something Miss Genevieve had told her when she first volunteered here: "Relay any information the people give you back to them. Make sure you've got it correct and solid."

"Um, okay. So, you're from somewhere not around here, maybe the other realm, surely not Cambelt or anywhere near it, and you left your father back home where . . . you fell through the floor before ending up here. You want to get home."

She nodded.

"And you are?"

"Azalea—Azalea Morroe."

"Okay, I'm Sunny. But, um, Azalea, I don't really know . . . I mean, I'm not sure how to get you home. I'm sorry."

"Oh. Okay." She sat still now and stared Sunny straight in the face, but her lip quivered the tiniest bit as Sunny patted her shoulder and stood up.

"You could talk to my boss, Miss Genevieve? She's wearing a brown dress today. If you find her, she might be able to help you."

"I already did. She didn't believe me." The next words seemed to spill out of Azalea's mouth almost as if she couldn't help herself. "She was kind of cold, um, like she didn't really want to help me. Is that normal? I mean, uh, could you say?"

So this was the girl her boss had mentioned earlier, who was supposedly delirious with exhaustion and could not be trusted, though she didn't seem out of her mind. Sunny frowned, spotting her boss several beds down. She could feel Azalea following her gaze to see Miss Genevieve cradling a baby in her arms, soothing its cries and whispering sweetly into its ear. She seemed perfectly warm and motherly just now.

"Um, I dunno, Azalea. Usually she's alright. I'm sorry she couldn't help you, though."

The girl nodded, allowing Sunny to make her way back through the crowd. This was not entirely a new scenario—refugees arrived here desperate to find loved ones and begged the volunteers to assist in a search for them rather frequently—but something about the girl's face made Sunny's chest squeeze, as if someone had encircled it with a rubber band.

Chapter Four

Azalea stared after the volunteer as she disappeared among the refugees. Dismay was settling about her like mist, distorting every other perception she had of this place. The sun was burning overhead now. Surely her father was sick with worry—maybe the administration at school had sent out an alert and the whole of Montero was on the lookout for her. But they would not find her, Azalea was certain now—certain that she had fallen into the other realm. She had not missed Sunny's choice of words: not another realm, but *the* other realm. She knew of the theory, regardless of whether or not she believed in Azalea's story.

There. She knew of something Azalea knew of too: they shared a common interest. She could definitely work from that, right? Persuade someone else that she really was from the other realm and get them to show her how to get back there? That could work. Right?

But even in her own head the conviction sounded hollow and shaky. She had already attempted to talk someone into this and the woman had basically tuned her out—seeming to think that adding "honey" to every sentence could trick Azalea into believing she cared, though the reason why she didn't was unclear.

And yet Azalea Morroe was not one to sit and wait for rescue. She was stuck here, but she had been struck with an idea: Her father was stuck in Montero, about to lose his job. She was here, so near to the place that his job-saving plan revolved around.

Why not make herself useful?

Chapter Five

"Go on home early, Sunny."

Miss Genevieve's chocolate hair had come loose from its bun, and the dark circles beneath her eyes had bolded tenfold, but she had the capacity for grace and was certainly compassionate and empathetic enough to sense her helper's exhaustion.

"Early, Miss? But—"

Miss Genevieve dismissed the feeble protestation with a wave of her hand and a little white lie. "Not many new arrivals just now. Take off while you can."

"But—"

"I insist." Seeing that Sunny was about to protest, Miss Genevieve added, "And don't come in tomorrow, either."

"Miss- -"

"Flood season'll be over just next week so hardly anyone's coming in anymore; you need a rest, and I can take it from here."

"I– "

"Just go, Sunny."

"Oh—alright."

"Good." A little smile flitted across Miss Genevieve's face.

But when she had started here, Sunny had been firmly informed that she had an obligation to make sure everyone was acting with compassion, even those who worked above her. "Um, Miss?"

"Yes, Sunny. What do you need now?"

"Well, I, uh, I heard from a refugee today that you didn't treat her with compassion. And you told me when I started here that I should make sure everyone was helping out to the best of their abilities regardless of status, so . . ." She trailed off, heart suddenly thundering in her chest. Miss Genevieve had never been cold to her, but now it looked like that might change.

"And who was this girl?"

"She was wearing a sweater with a green stripe across the front? Her name's—"

Her boss's face suddenly darkened. "She is the one I brought in this morning. You heard me say that she was delirious with hunger and exhaustion, did you not?"

"Well, yes, but she didn't—"

"And you believe me, do you not?"

"Well, Miss, with all due respect, she didn't seem to be—" Sunny had never seen Miss Genevieve like this, and could hardly believe her boldness, but something about that girl's face, which looked so much like Addi's, was urging her forward.

"Listen to me, Sunny. What else did she tell you?"

"What? I'm sorry, I don't—"

"Before she told you that I had not treated her with compassion, did she tell you any other lies?"

"Well, I'm not sure they were lies, Miss, but she did say that she had come from somewhere that was . . . not Cambelt."

"The other realm, perhaps?"

"What? I mean, uh, yes, actually. She did say that."

"Sunny, listen carefully. Between you and me, I did not treat this girl with compassion because she deserves none."

"What? That can't be right. When I first came here, you told me eve—"

"No. This is different. This girl, Sunny, or anyone who comes to you and tells you they are from the other realm and doesn't seem to be joking, they deserve no compassion. They are dangerous and do not mean well, and they should not be here. So stay out of their way."

"But Miss—"

"Go home now, Sunny." Miss Genevieve's face had softened a little, her exhaustion evident again. It was clear this conversation was over, and Sunny swallowed her further arguments and turned to leave.

But whatever her boss said, she could have her own opinions. And unlike Miss Genevieve, she wasn't planning on forcing anyone to believe them.

It barely took ten seconds for the restful times Genevieve had promised to Sunny to crash down around her ears. She had slung her bag back over her shoulder and was pushing open the side door when the girl in the green-and-white striped sweater who had insisted she was from the other realm came stumbling through the crowd.

"Hey! Hey, wait up!"

"Um—" Sunny seemed to have spent her entire day being cut off in the middle of a sentence.

"Listen, do you know how to get to Cambelt?"

The inquiry yanked Sunny roughly back into reality, one she usually didn't have to reenter until she'd gone back over the ridge toward home. The reality of Theo and Addi and Eli and Mama, of Jamone and her impending journey across the desert.

"I thought you wanted to go home? And Cambelt isn't your home?"

Azalea barely broke her stride. "Well. I've changed my mind, and Cambelt's where I need to be now. Do you know how to get there?"

"In theory, yes." Sunny knew the next question before it left the girl's tongue and winced.

"Could you take me?" Azalea seemed to realize what a tall order it was as soon as she said it, but Sunny's mouth seemed to have disconnected entirely from her brain and was talking away.

"Er—yeah. Yeah, I could—I'm actually heading there now. Is now a good time?"

It was Azalea's turn to look taken aback.

"I mean, I don't know how we'll get there," Sunny could hear herself saying. "But I'd be happy to take you, once we find a way."

"Do you have a car?"

"Um, what?"

"Do you have a car?"

"Do I have a *what*?"

"Uh, a car." Seeing the blank and confused expression, Azalea added, "It's a machine, that you drive, with four wheels?"

And then something clicked, a slow smile spreading across Sunny's face. This girl was joking!

"Oh, I get it! You mean an *automobile!*"

"I, um . . ." Azalea sighed. "Uh, yes. I do mean an automobile."

Sunny grinned wider than ever. Some demon was possessing her,

one that was whispering in her ear, *No time like the present. Mama didn't want you to warn her, did she?* and she did have a spare shirt folded in her rucksack, one she always brought to work in case of spilled soup or being called on to care for a baby. Maybe it was partly in rebellion against her boss' strangely xenophobic views, but the determination clicked in her head. "No, I haven't got a *car*."

"Well, there's one over there." And before Sunny could do anything but nod, her new friend strode over to the vehicle, picked up a large sand-colored rock from the edge of the lot, pulled herself up onto the automobile's top, and with a tremendous shattering of glass lobbed the rock right through the sunroof.

Chapter Six

"Oh my god. What are you doing?!" Sunny's voice had risen nearly an octave, all the color draining from her face.

The start of this adventure, like the start of all adventures, was intoxicating. A fire had ignited in the pit of Azalea's stomach, and she wasn't anywhere close to stopping what she'd just started. Her father had taught her two things about cars before they'd driven their ancient yellow buggy to the dump and walked home near midnight, making sure no one saw them (and thus ridding themselves of any tracking devices that Henry's work had tried to pin them with): how to hotwire with starter cables and how to fill the gas tank without a pump. This was in case they needed to steal a car or make a

A fire had ignited in the pit of Azalea's stomach, and she wasn't anywhere close to stopping what she'd just started.

quick escape of some sort.

"I've got us a car—an automobile, I mean."

With the red-painted metal mechanical cover open and the glass sunroof gleaming and exposed, the job had been easy. Once Azalea had seen the supplies—food, water, and gas—through the back windshield, she'd acted faster than even she had expected but didn't regret it in the slightest.

"I ... are you ..." Sunny sputtered, goggling at the battered red sedan. "Are you going to *steal it?*"

"Well, you haven't got any better ideas, have you? Besides, it's no longer in good shape."

"Only because ... I can't believe ..." She ran a hand up her face, gripping her hair exasperatedly in her fingers. "Do you know how to drive?"

This was something that Azalea always did, a skill she had learned at school and carried with her ever since—plowing forward with reckless abandon, high on the jitters of opportunity, drunk on the chance to give in to her impulses for once while also hiding vulnerability—two birds with one stone, and she was wired that way.

"Azalea, do *you* know how to drive?"

She glanced away, smiling rather sheepishly. "Well, no. But I know the *theory* ..."

"Oh, come on!"

But Azalea was quick to gloss over the flaw in her plan. "Listen. Here's what we'll do: help me clear the glass

and that big rock off the sunroof cover, then I'll slide it away and crawl into the car ... er, automobile. That way, I can let you in from the inside and we can figure out how to drive this thing."

"I ... oh, alright."

But it turned out that Azalea Morroe was too short to see clearly over the steering wheel in their new ride— they found that out after she pried the now slightly dented beige interior cover open with her fingers and tumbled as elegantly as possible into the seats below, checking for stray shards of glass in her hair. Sunny was taller but had never ridden in an automobile before in her life.

"Just press the pedal—yeah, that one—and turn the wheel the way you want to go—yeah, just like that— and we're off! There're a few other components, but we can improvise as we go along. It's perfect! I can drive sometimes, but don't expect the smoothest ride then!"

"Aren't there *keys*, or something? And what about fuel? Automobiles run on gasoline, right?"

"Yeah, well, I'm gonna hotwire the car—it doesn't really work yet—and then there's gas in the trunk we can fill the car with when it runs out."

"Uh, okay, but ... is that safe?"

"Yeah, my dad taught me how."

And so Sunny stood, staring out over the ridge and at the tiny trickle of refugees, wrapped in thick brown cloaks and looking like ants in the glaring sun, which was now high in the sky, as they made their way along the foot of the mountains west of the creek toward Ambergard. Azalea had popped the hood of the sedan and was working diligently inside it, fiddling with a screwdriver and both jumper cables at once. But Sunny wasn't interested in the mechanics of this endeavor—she was trying to stop the writhing in her stomach and the constricting sensation like an enormous rubber band around her chest.

Chapter Seven

Sunny was beginning to have doubts about her split-second decision-making skills. The demon had disappeared, and letting her mother stop her from making any plans was starting to look like a grave mistake— not like she would've won that battle anyway, but still. This was not exactly the most polished arrangement, and Azalea did not seem to have the most logical bent. Agreeing to do this had been the demon's last laugh. Theo, Addi, Eli, and Mama all needed her, and she was about to drive away from them—with barely any idea how—in a car along with the maniac who'd broken its sunroof.

"Alright, Sunny! The sun's gonna set soon, so we'd better get going!"

Azalea was abnormally cheerful and—though this was an entirely foreign land to her—seemed quite at home. Sunny was barely out her front door but too petrified at the prospect of this journey to move from the spot where she stood. The demon had taken her courage and signed her

up for this, and she couldn't back out now—the look on Azalea's face was too much like Addi's for that. The sand stretched endlessly before them, haze filling the air and shadowy shapes in the distance marking the mountains they would be forced to pass over on their way to the coast and the strait.

"Sunny, ready?" Azalea stood next to the passenger door, hands resting on the red metal roof.

Sunny bit her lip and swallowed hard. She wouldn't look back at Ambergard, not now. "Uh, yeah . . ."

Azalea beamed, disappearing into the automobile.

"Yeah. Let's go before I lose my nerve."

Ember Cube (Oil pastel)
Cyrus Kummer, 10
St. Louis, MO

Highlights from Stonesoup.com

From the Flash Contests

Weekly Creativity #142 | Flash Contest #29, March 2021
Write a story set somewhere you've never been. It could be set in outer space, Antarctica, or even an alternate reality!

 An excerpt from
Frank in the Galaxy
By Kimberley Hu, 8
Lake Oswego, OR

Chapter 1: Frank Got in Trouble

Frank was taking a walk around in the stained neighborhood (no idea why it was called that). Frank was so busy thinking about why the stained neighborhood was called the stained neighborhood that he accidentally bumped into the very fragile, most famous, awarded, and worshipped statue in all of the Jobbs Planet.

The statue of Frank Jobbie, Frank thought.

Then Frank realized that he didn't really care about the statue of Frank Jobbie. What was he thinking?!

Frank turned and saw a big crack in the statue of Frank Jobbie, or, as Frank liked to call it instead of saying "the statue of Frank Jobbie" so many times, TEE-ESS-OH-EF-JAY. That's just how you pronounce it. I mean, how you pronounce the letters. So, it would be TSOFJ, right? See, say TEE. What letter does that sound like? Yes, it sounds like the letter T. Now you get it.

Oh, no, no, no. Oops—not AGAIN, Frank thought very worriedly. Frank had already broken TSOFJ once three years ago on accident because Frank's spirit was strong. Frank was big and his hands were big, as were his feet, arms, legs, and just entire body. Except . . . his head. Well . . . it was SHORT. Frank's head was SHORT.

Luckily when Frank had broken TSOFJ, he had been forgiven and TSOFJ's broken part had been rebuilt. But the builders said, if Frank ever broke TSOFJ again, he would not be forgiven. And this time was that time. Frank was very alarmed. Frank wanted to run away as fast as he could, but he knew he couldn't. He had committed another crime. At least, breaking a part of TSOFJ was a crime.

Frank stood still with his mouth open and his legs startling. Frank knew there were secret security cameras around TSOFJ to make sure nothing happened to TSOFJ. It was too late. The security cameras had seen Frank, and Frank had no other choice than to stay still and accept it.

You can read the rest of Kimberley's story on our website: stonesoup.com/contests/

About the Stone Soup Flash Contests

Stone Soup holds a flash contest during the first week of every month. The month's first Weekly Creativity prompt provides the contest challenge. Submissions are due by midnight on Sunday of the same week. Up to five winners are chosen for publication on our blog. The winners, along with up to five honorable mentions, are announced in the following Saturday newsletter. Find all the details in the Activities and Contests sections of our website.

Honor Roll

Welcome to the Stone Soup Honor Roll. Every month, we receive submissions from hundreds of kids from around the world. Unfortunately, we don't have space to publish all the great work we receive. We want to commend some of these talented writers and artists and encourage them to keep creating.

STORIES

Isa Cramer, 10
Ciara Feng, 12
En-Yu Liu, 12

PERSONAL NARRATIVES

Joshua Fields, 11
Lindsay Gao, 9
Perry Garon, 12
Jessica Yao, 11

POETRY

Grayson Cassell, 14
Ahana Chandra, 12
Lucy Fleisher, 9
Lucas Hinds, 12
Deekshita Joshi, 8
Hannah Rice, 8
Aya Sakurai, 13
Ananya Venkateswaran, 8

ART

Elyse Bambrough, 9
Mattea Bambrough, 7
Analise Braddock, 9
Max Renfrow, 10
Noor Syed, 11
Celine Xie, 6